The Springridge Incident

Sandra K-Horn

For my Granddaughter
Evelyn

This book was inspired by an incident that
occurred in 2006. The names
of the principles have been changed as well
as the city.

1

The Ghost House

The teens tiptoed as they neared their goal. They crept along the peeling white picket fence that seemed to hold back the eight-foot-tall privets that barricaded The Ghost House. This Halloween was dark. A cloud masked the moon. No streetlights lit their path. Tricker treaters were all home by now, so there was no sound except the wind blowing through the trees lining the street and faint chimes from a neighbor's yard.

Madison led, using her phone to light the way. To be the one who organized the girls would surprise no one. She was the captain of their field hockey team and the leader of their close-knit group. Ashley walked in the middle, with April lagging. All three wore tennis shoes, but the leaves and residue on the uneven sidewalk made their steps crunch as they tiptoed along.

They reached the only gap in the fence. A cord held the gate open, and the black, willowy vines covering its arch swayed in the breeze. Madison turned to shush her friends. At five foot eight, she had to duck to go through the opening. Just as the girls stepped onto their target property, the clouds parted to reveal a pale blue moon. The shadows of long tentacle tree branches suggested movement on the lawn and the front of The Ghost House. All three girls gasped as they stood on the walkway. The face of the grayish house had two square windows on the second floor and a larger one on the first. All were dark. The porch was to their right, with a small window above its protruding roof. April whispered. "I hope no one's home."

"Seriously, where would they go?" Ashley said.

"The graveyard?" Madison giggled.

The old slate walkway was broken and created uneven levels. It spanned from the gate opening across the front of the house to the porch. The girls held on to each other to avoid tripping. All three girls held their breaths as they crossed to the porch in front of the house.

"What is that smell?" Ashley said.

"It smells like manure," Madison said.

Ashley squeaked. She froze.

Madison turned. "What?"

"Something just brushed my legs!"

April put her hand out. "Ashley, the grass is really high. See the white tips?"

"Look!" Ashley was looking up at one of the second-story windows.

"What, Ashley?"

"Did a curtain move up there? Is that window open?"

April whispered. "I don't see anything."

A board complained as Madison stepped on the first of two porch steps. "Jesus!"

"Keep going!"

Madison skipped the second step. Ashley avoided the first step, only to cause a squawk on the second. April tiptoed to the edge of both steps to prevent making sounds.

The three girls stood on the porch that slanted toward the house. Checking to ensure their phones were ready for all-important selfies, they posed. With their other hands, they formed fists. Whispering together, "One, two, three," they banged on the front door, then soaped their initials on the glass. Laughing, they took their selfies. Madison flew off the porch with Ashley right behind. April, shorter and not so nimble, ran down the stairs.

They paused as they neared the fence opening. "Damn! My picture didn't come out well! I only got half my face! I need to go back."

"No!" Said Ashley. "I got you in my picture, Madison. I'll share it with you."

Pop! Pop! Pop! The girls screamed. Three more pops exploded after they flew down the street. Ashley heard April groan as she ran toward the car, and her hands slapped the ground. She glanced back, and she saw April on her hands and knees. Ashley dashed back to help April. "Did you trip?"

April shook her head no. As Madison reached the corner, she saw Ashley putting her arm around April, attempting to pull her up. She sprinted to her friends, got on the other side of April, and half dragged her to the car. After Ashley swung the sedan's rear door open, both girls lowered April into the backseat. Ashley looked at her hand in the interior lights. "Oh, my God! She's bleeding!"

Madison, noticing the blood on Ashley's hand, turned to see April on her side, panting. Her breathing was shallow. "Let's get out of here! Call 911!"

"Where should I tell them to go?" Ashley fumbled for her phone as she struggled to get it out of the pocket of her jeans.

"We're close to downtown. We'll meet the ambulance in the parking lot of Shake Shack."

The emergency vehicle was pulling into the Shake Shack as Madison parked her car. She flung open her car door, stood, and screamed, "She's in here! April's hurt!"

The ambulance stopped at the back of Madison's car. Ashley ran up to the driver's side and yelled. "She's bleeding!"

The EMTs split up. One hurried to the passenger side of the car. The other to the back of the ambulance. The EMT yanked the rear car door open and barked, "We'll need the backboard!"

April was awake and crying. The pungent odor of blood and urine greeted the EMT as he leaned in to examine her. Blood was on the seat and soaking through her jacket. "What's your name?"

"April."

"April, we're going to take care of you. Can you tell me what happened?"

"Happened?"

"Okay, April. There's some blood on the seat. I'm going to

pat you down to see where the blood is coming from. Is that okay with you?"

April nodded and whispered, "Yes."

The EMT yelled to Madison. "Push your seat up as far as it can go."

Madison pushed the lever that moved the seat forward. The EMT moved the front seat up on his side. He climbed back in and knelt on the floor. "I'm going to start now, April. Can you tell me what happened?"

He started close to the base of her neck, patting her back and side, and then stretched her legs out. He turned to the second EMT standing by with the gurney. "It's not a back wound. We need gauze to stay the bleeding on her right side."

Crying and gasping, April said, "We were taking selfies at The Ghost House."

The EMT said, "You guys still doing that?"

He then patted April, starting at her sternum and down her front. "There's no sign of bleeding in the front."

"We heard loud bangs like firecrackers and ran."

"April, I'm going to lift your shirt to put a pressure bandage on your side." To the other EMT, "We'll need a neck brace and the backboard. Firecrackers? April, we need to get you out of here. Lie still. We're going to slide the backboard underneath you."

April tried to turn to sit up. "No, I can... Oh. I can't move my legs. Madison, Ashley, I can't feel my legs!"

"April, I want you to stay as you are. We'll take care of you."

The EMT crawled back out of the car, lifted April's legs, and slid the board under her. The two EMTs eased April out of the vehicle. Once they placed the board on the cot, they rolled her over onto her back and put a neck brace on her. The EMT instructed the girls to call April's parents and tell them to meet them at the hospital. Once April was in the ambulance, the driver stopped the administering EMT.

"One of the other girls said they heard firecrackers."

"Call it in. Those weren't firecrackers. It was gunshots. This girl was shot."

2

Investigation of the shooting

"Possible shots fired on Brueberry Lane by Sweet Memories Garden Cemetery."

"Copy that, car 5 reporting."

Officer Lydia Pabana switched on her siren and headed down Main Street. Springridge was not a big town, so she'd be two minutes away. Most likely, it would be just kids playing with firecrackers on Halloween. Common occurrence.

She turned into Brueberry Lane and coasted to see if people in the neighborhood were out in their yards. Passing the two-story eclectic homes, she rolled down her window and felt a cool wind smelling of falling leaves. She could hear faint sounds, possibly a television too loud, and a dog barking on the next street. The dispatcher could have given her an address.

"Do you have an address on Brueberry?"

"The report came from 105 Brueberry. Trudy Anderson."

"Okay, thanks."

Trudy Anderson. Regular church lady who watched her street and reported anything amiss. Anything. Pabana pulled her vehicle in front of Trudy's house. She opened her car door, put on her cap, and walked to Trudy's front door. The lights were on in the front room, so Lydia knew Trudy was awake. She rang the bell. Lydia smiled, knowing Trudy had already checked her Ring camera.

"Officer Pabana."

Pabana tipped her cap. "Hi, Mrs. Anderson. Can you tell me what direction you think the gunshots came from?"

Trudy nodded. "The end of the street by the cemetery, I think. You know how sound bounces around. But I'm pretty sure."

"Thanks, Mrs. Anderson. Did you hear anything else?"

"No, I don't think so. Maybe some talking."

"Thanks again. Have a good evening."

"You too."

As she walked to her vehicle, her radio squawked. "Pabana."

"There's a report of a gunshot wound at Mercy Hospital."

"Ten-four."

Ten minutes later, she pulled into the Emergency area and parked in a reserved parking slot. She scanned the emergency area. Not too busy. Only three beds were occupied. There were two teenage girls with their heads together in the waiting area.

Addressing the emergency nurse, she said, "Pam, I got a call about a gunshot report?"

"Yeah, the EMTs rushed a girl in here about forty-five minutes ago. They just took her in for a CT scan. Those two girls came in right after they brought the girl. Her parents are in number one."

"Okay, thanks."

Pabana approached the girls. "Hi girls, I'm Officer Pabana. Were you involved with the shooting that happened tonight?"

The two teens looked at each other. The taller of the two answered. "Yes."

Pabana took out her notepad and asked their names. The shorter girl asked, "Are we in trouble?"

Pabana said. "I'm not sure what happened. Until you tell me, I can't really answer that."

The taller girl straightened in her seat. Her voice took on a haughty tone. "My name is Madison Wernock. I'm not sure we should talk to you."

The other girl said, "I'm Ashley McCarthy." Her eyes were already red and swollen. "I called my mom. She's on her way."

Pabana looked around. "Okay. Good. Ladies, let's go into this room over here to talk."

She motioned to Pam, the emergency nurse, and led them into a side room, where she closed the door. "Tell me about yourselves."

She motioned for them to sit in two chairs next to each other at a table and pulled one out for herself. She sat directly across from them.

Again, Madison took the lead. "We're seniors. We play on the Field Hockey team."

"You guys have been having a pretty good season."

Both smiled and nodded.

Pabana paused to let them go silent for a minute. "Do you feel comfortable telling me what happened tonight?"

Ashley said, "Can we wait for my parents?"

"Absolutely. Madison, have you called your parents?"

"My parents are out of town."

"You could FaceTime with them," Ashley said.

Madison tilted her head and made a "Are you serious face?".

A knock. Pam opened the door and stuck her face in. "One of the girls' parents is here."

"Could you tell them we're in here?"

Two adults came into the room. Their eyes went straight to Ashley, then to the officer. The woman went to Ashley and asked if she was okay. Officer Pabana stood. "Mr. and Mrs. McCarthy, I'm Officer Lydia Pabana." She moved around the table and extended her hand. "Please join us."

"I'm not sure that is in my daughter's best interest," Mr. McCarthy said, taking her hand.

"Mr. McCarthy, I'm not here to get anyone in trouble," Pabana said. "I'm just trying to figure out how a young girl was shot."

The McCarthys looked at each other. Mrs. McCarthy nodded. "Officer, we know you are doing the right thing here. I'm a lawyer. I will stop the girls if I find them incriminating themselves."

"That's fine."

The adults all sat at the table. "Ashley and Madison, will you tell me what happened?"

"We went to The Ghost House to take selfies. As we were leaving, we heard firecrackers. Twice." Madison said.

"But they weren't firecrackers."

Ashley and Madison both slowly shook their heads.

"Okay, what happened after you heard the gunshots?"

"We ran."

"But April fell."

"April, was the girl who was shot?"

Both girls nodded.

Ashley, wiping away tears, said. "When April fell, I thought she tripped. I stopped to help her up. She was having trouble walking."

"I went back to help them, and we made it to the car. We helped her get into the backseat." Madison said.

"Okay. Good. Go on."

"When I got into the front seat, I noticed blood on my hands. I turned to April, and she was lying on her side. She was hardly breathing."

"I told Ashley to call 911 and to have the ambulance meet us at the Shake Shack."

"Why? Did you think whoever shot at you would come after you?"

Madison said. "I-I don't know. I just wanted to get out of there."

"Okay. So the ambulance met you at the Shake Shack."

Ashley bit her lip. Madison was teary. "Yes."

Pabana grabbed the Kleenex box on the counter and put it on the table between the girls.

"We yelled for them to help April," Ashley said. "Two of the guys ran to the car. One of them climbed in the backseat with her."

Madison said, "He asked me to pull the driver's seat up as far as it would go."

"Girls, you are doing really well."

"The guy pulled out a backboard and the cot thing."

Madison touched Ashley's arm. "The driver checked to see if we were okay. We both said yes."

"That's when we heard April scream. She couldn't feel her legs."

Both girls were weeping.

Pabana took in a deep breath. "Okay, girls. Good. I need to ask you. Do you know where the shots came from?"

Madison said, "We didn't think anyone was home. It was all dark. We even said we thought no one was home."

Ashley said. "We went to the front door, knocked, took

selfies, and ran down the walk. Madison didn't like her selfie and wanted to turn back, but I said she would share mine. Then we heard the firecrackers."

"We turned and ran."

"That's when April fell."

"But you didn't see anyone."

Both girls shook their heads and said no.

Pabana looked at her watch. "It's past midnight." To the McCarthys, she said, "I'll bet you would like to get Ashley home. Before you leave, let me have phone numbers if we need to sit and talk again."

Mrs. McCarthy said, "Madison, are you okay to drive home?"

Madison nodded. "Wait, you're not staying at the McCarthy's home?" the officer said.

Madison's eyebrows arched. "I'm eighteen. My parents believe I can take of myself."

Pabana took a moment to write her notes and considered the information the girls gave her. She needed to talk to April if the doctors and her parents let her. If she returned to Brueberry Lane tonight, she didn't think she would see much. She needed to talk to her supervisor about what he wanted her to do.

3

April

April was rushed into the emergency room at Mercy Hospital. On her left, a person was taking her blood pressure. On her right, another was gently touching her side. A doctor told someone to schedule a CAT scan STAT. She was trying to answer questions someone was asking close to her head. At the same time, a doctor asked her if she could feel this. April lifted her head to look at him by her feet. "What do you want me to feel?"

Her mom and dad rushed into the room after the medical people replaced the pressure bandage on her side.

"Do I have a bullet in me?" April, weeping, asked the doctor.

"We will see more with the CAT scan," he said.

"Dad, why can't I feel my legs if the bullet went in my side?"

"April, are you in a lot of pain?" Her father said. His eyes were wide and damp. His face was pale.

"My side hurts, but not as much as it did in the car."

The doctor glanced at her mom and dad and pulled up a stool. "You have a lot of swelling right now, so the CAT scan will tell us more. We don't know yet about the weapon used, but judging from the entrance wound, it might have been a 22 caliber. What that means is the bullet might have tumbled or become what's called a wadcutter and hit your spinal cord."

Her mom gasped.

"What we need to see is where the bullet is and how much damage it did. Does that all make sense to you?"

April nodded despite her confusion and wiped tears from

her face.

"Okay, I'll be back. The CAT scan should be available in a few minutes."

Dr. Simmons, April's dad, walked out with the doctor.

April closed her eyes. Mrs. Simmons's voice was tearful and strained. April could tell she was trying to stay calm enough to talk to her. "How are Madison and Ashley?"

"I think they're okay."

"Typical."

April, concentrating on lying still, said, "Are you blaming them for what happened tonight?"

Her mom cleared her throat. "Are you in a lot of pain, honey?"

"My hips and side ache. I have a headache."

Then April remembered Jedidiah, the EMT, said Madison and Ashley were coming to the hospital. "Are Madison and Ashley here at the hospital?"

"I don't think you should see them right now."

"Why?"

"Look what they did to you."

April thought her mom's thinking was a little off. "Mom, they didn't shoot me."

"They're responsible."

April swallowed. "Can I see them, please?"

A nurse came in to tell them they were taking her for tests. April was relieved.

The nurse and an attendant put up the sides of the bed and started wheeling her down the hall. April had never seen a CAT scan. It looked like an enormous tube. Another medical person, a dark-haired lady with glasses that magnified her eyes, asked how she was doing, her name, and birthdate. Since someone had already cut away her shirt, all April had on was a sheet on top of her. "I'm cold."

"Tell you what. As soon as we see what's going on, I'll find a nice warm blanket to put on you."

April smiled but didn't feel it.

"These are headphones you can wear. What music would you like? We can do Demi Lovato or Taylor Swift."

She helped April put the headphones on.

"Okay, I'm going to put your arms up over your head so we can get a clear picture of what's going on, okay?"

She took April's arms and stretched them over her head.

"Okay, April. Don't move."

The machine whirled and clicked. Taylor's familiar voice kept April from becoming anxious. The lady in the adjoining room spoke to her and let her know she was doing well. The tech's voice was soothing. April relaxed, wondering if Madison and Ashley were still at the hospital or her mom had chased them home. She daydreamed if she moved her fingers, would she mess everything up?

Five songs later, the lady said she was done.

As the tech took the headphones, April asked her how she was. The tech smiled the kind of smile someone gives a person when they know they won't answer. "Your doctor will let you know after he looks at the film. Here's that warm blanket I promised you."

The blanket's warmth hugged her shoulders and chest.

Again, a nurse came in with an attendant. "We're going to take you back to a temporary room close to the ER so you can see your parents."

"Will the doctor tell me what's going to happen?"

Again, that smile. "He'll be with you as soon as he can."

April waited in the temporary room, staring at the ceiling. She wished someone would come. Finally, her dad stepped into her room, trailed by her mom. April turned her head to talk to them. "Did you talk to the doctor?"

"Yes, April. We talked about transferring you to the Midtown Medical Center."

"Why?"

"The bullet traveled and is close to your spinal cord. I'd rather have a specialist look at you. There isn't one here at Mercy."

"Can't one come here?"

"The doctor will let you know you have a long road in front of you. MSU has a wonderful rehab center that can get you started down the right path."

"I don't understand, Dad."

The door swung open again. A husky man walked in

wearing a stethoscope. He differed from the emergency doctor April had seen before. He stepped over to her bed and reached out his hand. "Hi, April. I'm Dr. Rakko. You got yourself into a bit of trouble. Elizabeth, can you raise her bed? Not too much."

The nurse took the controller and raised the bed a bit.

"Better?"

April said, "Yes."

The doctor placed the film he had carried in on a small whiteboard. Turning on a light, the picture of April's torso lit up. He pointed. "Here is your lumbar area. This is your spinal cord. This bright spot is the bullet. Whoever shot you used a standard 22 bullet, which is a good thing. It did less damage than a hollow point. Here is where the bullet entered. You must have turned to the side. The bullet, once it entered your side, moved to the L1 area."

April's voice shook a little. "Are you going to get it out?"

"Your dad here wants to have you moved to Midtown Medical Center. We don't have a neurosurgeon here who has an orthopedic specialty. That's what your dad wants for you. And I don't blame him. We will keep you comfortable until your dad can arrange transportation to Midtown. Now, a police officer has been waiting to speak to you. With your parents' permission, I will let her know you can talk to her."

April looked at her mom and dad. Both nodded.

The police officer seemed weighed down by all the equipment she carried around her waist. She shook hands with the adults as she introduced herself to them. She then turned her attention to April. "Hi, April. My name is Lydia Pabana. I've talked to your friends about what happened, but I also wanted to talk to you. Can you tell me what happened?"

"I don't remember hardly anything after the firecrackers. Well, now I know they were gunshots. I remember my side hurting suddenly. It hurt like I had been running for a long time. It was so painful I fell. I remember Madison and Ashley telling me we had to get to the car. The next thing I remember is the EMT telling me not to move. He and his partner were going to put a backboard underneath me to get me out of the backseat of the car. I wanted to curl up or straighten up, anything to stop the pain that was burning my side and eating up my whole body. The EMT helped me straighten my legs out and then asked if it was okay for him to check out if I had wounds. I said yes, but I didn't really understand why I would have any wounds. Once I was on the backboard, I tried to move my legs. I couldn't. That's when I got terrified. I yelled to Madison and Ashley that I couldn't move my legs.

I remember flying through the air, or it seemed like it. That's when the guys were putting me in the ambulance.

I remember one of the EMTs introducing himself. His name was Jedidiah. He told me he was going to put an IV in me. I was cold. Jedidiah said to the other guy I was going into shock. Jedidiah told me I was going to feel a pinch. The other guy told him he was going to start fluids and that I had lost a lot of blood.

I asked Jedidiah what the other guy's name was. He said, David. David was reporting to the hospital and telling them about me and gunshots. That's when I realized the firecrackers weren't firecrackers.

I asked if Madison and Ashley were okay. Jedidiah said David had checked them out, and they were fine. They were going to call my parents and meet us at the hospital. He also said to leave the oxygen on and relax."

"April, why were you there?"

April looked down and made a face. "We wanted to take selfies that we went to the Ghost House and completed the senior tradition."

"Okay, thanks, April. That's all. I'll bet your parents would like you to get some rest." Officer Pabana patted April's hand and smiled at her parents.

"Thank you for letting me talk to her."

She left April's room and sat in the waiting room to write down some notes.

4

Ben

Officer Lydia Pabana was disappointed. After finishing her reports, her supervisor told her she should brief a detective and go home. Her shift was 10:30 PM to 7 AM, and the supervisor wasn't about to okay overtime for this investigation.

None of the detectives were in when she was ready to leave, so she put her report in Detective Darnell Bennet's in-file with a note that read ASAP. She knew they would cover this in the morning briefings.

Cocky and well-known in town, Detective Bennet was one of the two detectives on Springridge's police force. He carried himself in the familiar former football player manner, balancing his broad shoulders and once slim hips as he swaggered to a chair. The Officer of the Day, Peter Jonesy, briefed the nine veteran officers covering the day shift in Springridge. Jonesy described Halloween pranks reported and assigned officers to look into the complaints. He outlined the shooting on Brueberry Lane and told Officer Bob Sinema to accompany Bennet to the scene.

As they walked to Sinema's vehicle, Bennet said, "You know, this public relations shtick of the mayor and chief is ridiculous. My car is more comfortable."

Sinema shrugged. "No, big deal, Bennet. It establishes a presence."

"Heard anything about The Ghost House?"

"Yeah, the guy who lives there was a few years before my class in high school. Strange guy."

"I knew about him and his mother, but he was younger, so I didn't pay much attention. Isn't she the lady who used to talk to herself in the grocery store and sing while she walked down the street?"

Sinema yawned. "Yeah. When we were in high school, she used to go around the neighborhood with a parrot on her shoulder. The bird squawked at kids when they passed. Don't think it said anything. Didn't she call him Sonny?"

"Who the parrot?"

"No, her son."

"Okay. I remember now. Sonny Franklin. Didn't he, a couple of years ago, not let the police in after his mother died?"

"Yeah, it was sad. The neighbors complained of the smell. Chris Petrick and I had to get Barb Yarnell, the librarian, to come over and talk him into letting the coroner into the house."

They pulled up in front of Franklin's house.

As Bennet ducked to avoid the growth that arched the yard's entrance, he paused to take in the house's overgrown yard and mossy siding. "Boy, it looks even worse in daylight."

Sinema exhaled, "Yeah. Well, let's get this done."

The two police officers walked up to the front porch. When Bennet stepped on the first stair, it gave and felt mushy under his foot. "Damn. Be careful of the step."

The second step squeaked as he moved to the slanting porch. Sinema knocked. Both men stood listening. Sinema rapped on the door again. "Mr. Franklin, open up. Police."

No answer.

Bennet tried with a sharper pounding.

No answer.

"I wonder if he's over at the library," Sinema said. "He works there. We should go over and check."

Bennet made a face. "I think we should try for a search warrant. We could use the girls' testimony as probable cause."

Sinema nodded. "But while you get the warrant, I'm going to the library to see if he's there."

They turned to go down the creaking steps. As they walked in front of the house, Bennet put out his hand to stop Sinema. "Wait. I saw a curtain move."

Both retraced their steps. Bennet pounded again. "Come on,

Mr. Franklin. We need to talk to you about last night," Sinema said.

The door squeaked open.

The daylight revealed a man of average height. His hair was short and neat. He was wearing khakis and a light blue shirt. "What do you want?"

Sinema said, "Mr. Franklin, can we come in? This is Detective Bennet, and we have to ask you some questions."

Stepping forward, Ben squinted in the sunlight. "About what?"

"Last night. Those girls you shot at," Bennet said.

Sinema put his hand up to stop Bennet. "Can we come in and talk?"

"You came when my mom died."

Sinema nodded. "Yes. I got Mrs. Yarnell to help."

"I remember. Okay, come in."

He backed in but kept his eyes on Bennet.

The lemon polish-scented living room was neat and tidy, with little clutter. The rug showed tracks of being vacuumed.

"Mr. Franklin, what happened last night?"

Ben shifted. He folded his arms; his chin was down, but his focus remained on Bennet.

"Sir?"

"The kids kept knocking. Even after trick or treat was over."

"What time did the last knock occur?"

"Half-past eleven. I'm going to work today. I needed to go to bed." Sinema noticed Franklin's right hand was tapping his left arm.

"So why aren't you at work?" Bennet said.

"I work at 10."

"Mr. Franklin, what happened after the last knock occurred?" Sinema said.

Ben turned to him. "I had my rifle to scare them away. They looked like they were coming back. They trespassed. I didn't even have my light on, so the kids wouldn't come to trick or treat."

"You shot out the front window?"

"No. From my bedroom window. But I didn't aim at them. I just wanted to scare them away."

Detective Bennet took a step forward. "Come on, Sinema.

Just tell him he shot a girl."

Almost cowering, Ben took a step back. "What? No, I didn't. I shot at the bushes. I wanted them to leave me alone and stop knocking on my doors and windows. Kids egg my house. Two days ago, they dumped manure."

"Ben Franklin, we have to arrest you for felonious assault. The girl is in the hospital."

Sinema, about the same height as Franklin, stepped forward to turn him around to handcuff him. Franklin submitted easily to his gesture. Bennet took out his Miranda card and started reading it to him.

"…If you cannot afford an attorney, one will be appointed for you. *Do you understand the rights I have just read to you? With these rights in mind, do you wish to speak to me?*"

To Sinema, Franklin said, "Yes, but those girls were trespassing."

"Let's go down to the station. How about I call Mrs. Yarnell and tell her you won't be at work today?"

Franklin had his head down, but he nodded.

***

Ben Franklin paced in the interrogation room. All of what happened to him in the last twenty-four hours was unfair. He was placed in the back of the police car by a guy he had known from high school. The other one had helped him when his mom died. *What was his name? Sinema, yeah, Sinema. Officer Sinema.* He said he would call the library to let them know he wouldn't be at work this time. Bennet said a girl was hurt. He felt bad someone was hurt, but he had to protect his property. Ben kept a steady beat with his right hand on his left arm.

The officers had taken him to the Springridge jail, sat him in a room, and left him there. He kept telling them in the car and walking into the police station he was protecting his house. Officer Sinema said to stop talking. Bennet kept badgering him about shooting a girl. Officer Sinema told Bennet to let him be.

He had sat in this room for a long time. Restless, he walked back and forth. He had to pee. Finally, the door swung open. Officer Sinema came in with another police officer.

"Mr. Franklin. Why don't you sit down?"

"Officer, I'd like to go to the restroom."

"Okay, come on. Would you like some water or coffee when you get back?"

"Yes, water would be good."

When they returned, both officers sat down with him. "Do you like to be called Sonny or Ben?"

"Ben."

"Ben, this is Officer Petrick. I don't know if you remember him."

Ben looked at Petrick for a brief time and shook his head. "No."

"Ben, do you want to call an attorney?"

"I don't know any attorneys."

"Can you afford one, Ben?" Officer Petrick said.

Ben thought for a moment. "I don't think so."

"Would you notify the county court he needs a court-appointed attorney?"

Officer Petrick stood and left the room.

"Ben, wait for your attorney before you say anything else."

"When do you think that will happen?"

"Tomorrow."

"Can I go home?"

"I'm afraid you'll be here overnight, Ben."

"This doesn't make sense. I was protecting my home. People were egging and throwing manure at my house."

"What's going to happen, Ben, is the attorney will meet with you in the morning. You'll be arraigned tomorrow afternoon, and bail might be assigned then."

"Then can I go home?"

"You and your attorney will talk about that tomorrow."

5

10TV News

Marcie Reynolds, morning to news and special production producer, watched as news anchors Killian Gregory and David Sweeney delivered the Columbus Noon News. Killian looked into the camera and reported, "A Springridge teen was shot on Halloween night. Harriet Parkins has the story."

The monitor cut to a video shot of Ben Franklin's house. The video started at the property's entrance and zoomed through the fence's opening to show the house and yard. Harriet's voice is heard in the video.

"April Simmons thought she and her two friends, Madison Wernock and Ashley McCarthy, were just carrying out the senior tradition of knocking on the door of the house called The Ghost House when shots rang out. Benjamin Franklin, the homeowner, had had it. He was sick of kids knocking on his door and windows. Simmons was shot and is at Springridge's Mercy Hospital. Dr. Malaki Simmons, her father, had this to say. "

The monitor showed Dr. Simmons in a hallway at Mercy Hospital.

"The kids were harmless. They knocked on the front door and took selfies. If the guy was so bothered by it, he should have left for the evening."

"Was this a senior tradition?"

"Look, he should have called the police, not shot at the girls."

"Thank you, Dr. Simmons. This is Harriet Parkins for 10TV News."

Killian's image returned to the monitor. "Franklin will appear before a judge today on three counts of felonious assault." She turned to David. "You know that's a shame. There's a lot wrong there."

David agreed and then introduced Paul Schultz with the weather.

As she walked out of the control room, Marcie nodded in agreement.

6

April

After Officer Pabana left, a nurse asked how April was doing.

"My side hurts."

"The doctor left instructions for pain medication so I can give you some relief."

The nurse reached for the intravenous tubing and attached another smaller bag to the hook above April's bed.

"April, I will have the transport here for you tomorrow," her dad said. He leaned over and kissed the top of her head. "I'll meet you there. Love you."

"Honey, I will send some things with your dad so you're more comfortable. I love you." Her mom took her hand. "I'll see you tomorrow afternoon."

April was asleep even before they left the hospital.

***

April woke several times during the night. Sometimes, it was a nurse checking her vitals. Sometimes, it was the pain that woke her. Another time, April saw the nurse empty a pee bag. In the morning, she woke as her breakfast of broth and yellow jello arrived. The nurse who brought it in moved the tray close to her and raised her bed slightly. "Nurse, do you know where my phone is?"

"No, honey. I don't. But since you came in through emergency last night, I imagine one of your parents took it home with them? Did you have a purse?"

"No, I had it in my pocket."

"I imagine that's what happened then." The nurse looked in the drawers and small closet. "Looks like everything is empty. Don't you worry now. We'll wrap you in warm blankets to take you up to Columbus. Here's the remote for the TV. We'll let you know when the transport is here."

***

Her dad was at the Medical Center when she arrived. He walked with her as they took her to her room. "The doctors are looking at the CAT scan films now. I'll wait with you until they come in so we can discuss what they want to do. How's your pain?"

"They gave me some pain medication before I left this morning. So far, it's okay. Where's mom?"

"She was pretty emotional last night, April. She'll be here later today. I suggested she keep her appointments this morning. The routine will calm her down."

Together, they stared at the television monitor. "I never realized how bad morning shows were," her dad said.

"Dad, could you ask mom to bring my phone?"

He smiled. "Going through withdrawal?"

She laughed. "Well, yeah."

"Okay, I'll try. Your mom was upset about your friends pulling you into this silly game."

"My friends didn't pull me into anything. People do this all the time. You and Mom knew what we were going to do. It's a senior tradition."

"Okay, but no one has gotten hurt before."

"Yeah."

A knock on the door interrupted them. A man and woman came into April's room. Both had white coats and stethoscopes. The man was Indian, and the woman was African American.

"I am Dr. Duttagupta, and this is Dr. Khumalo." He nodded to my dad. "Dr. Simmons."

My dad nodded back.

"We looked at the pictures of your daughter's spinal area. The bullet is pressing up against the L2 vertebrae. At this time, we will not do surgery."

"Why not?" Her dad's voice had changed from when he was talking to April to a louder, lower tone.

"This seemed to be a low-energy projectile. It is believed that nonsurgical management is preferred unless there is progressive neurological deterioration to the spinal cord, persistent CSF fistula, or a migration of the bullet within the spinal canal."

"What are our next steps, then?" Her dad followed up.

Dr. Khumalo spoke, "April is to rest. Healing is paramount. We will watch as the swelling goes down." She spoke directly to April. "Your body is doing its best to protect itself from further injury, April, so we will do our best to help it. After we see how it heals, we will make further decisions."

April put her hand up. Dr. Khumalo smiled. "Yes, April."

"When will I be able to walk again?"

Dr. Duttagupta answered. "We shall see."

7

Springridge Gazette

Girl in Critical Condition During Halloween Prank

By Robert Cunningham

(Springridge, Ohio) Someone shot at three Springridge High School girls, wounding one of them after the girls had carried out the controversial senior tradition of knocking on the door of the house teens called The Ghost House.

A man who lives in the house, Benjamin (Sonny) Franklin, was arrested Tuesday in the shooting of 18-year-old April Simmons the night before. Franklin told reporters he wanted to stop kids from knocking on his door and wanted to chase off the trespassers so he could be left alone. He had no intention of hurting anyone.

Simmons remained in critical condition Wednesday at Midtown Brain and Spine Hospital at the Midtown University Medical Center.

April's father, Dr. Malaki Simmons, told reporters that April was resting but could not move her lower extremities.

Franklin's home, near the Sweet Memories Gardens Cemetery, had a reputation among local teens for being haunted. The Springridge High School students had a senior tradition of daring each other to knock on the door or go in the yard for years, Springridge Police Chief Carl Perton said.

Simmons and her two friends had knocked on Franklin's door and were running away when they thought they heard firecrackers. Simmons fell, and the other two girls carried her to their car. The other two girls, Ashley McCarthy and Madison Wernock, were not injured.

Hundreds gathered on the high school football field Thursday night for a vigil for Simmons, a field hockey player at the school of about 1800 students.

Police said Franklin, an IT person with the Springridge Library who lives alone, told investigators he aimed at the ground. He wanted to scare the girls away. Franklin, 35, will appear before a judge on three counts of felonious assault. His bond was set at $650,000.

Records show that the rifle had belonged to Franklin's father.

8

April

April leafed through her Pre-Cal text. Looking up at the TV in her hospital room, she clicked it on and off. Her copy of *Macbeth* haunted her as it rested on the hospital tray. She was already more than a week behind in school. The doctors told her that this was the most challenging time. She had to rest and wait until the swelling went down before any decisions about her rehab could take place. It was between breakfast and lunch, and visiting hours seemed years away. Besides that, her mom and dad only came to visit. Her friends weren't allowed. Her mom was still laying the blame on them for her being in the hospital. She looked at the basket of get-well cards from her school. She didn't even recognize the names of some kids who sent them. Her IB* Lit class made a poster for her, but it's too big for her hospital room. She'd see it again when she got home. At least her mom returned her phone, but all her friends were in classes.

I'd be in IB Euro right now. Why doesn't the swelling go down?

She pressed the remote to lift the bed higher, then used her arms to push herself into a higher sitting position. April twisted her torso so she could reach her iPad. She looked up *No Fear Shakespeare. I think I left off in Act Three scene* —-A white hot pain shot up her spine and up the back of her skull. "Oh, geez!"

She pushed the remote to lower the bed again. The pain did not ease. Shaking, she wondered what she had done. Tears running down her face, she repositioned herself. She shifted her weight, hoping whatever she did would correct itself. A cold sweat broke out on her chest and arms, and her stomach soured. *What if I made things worse?* Breathing to steady herself, she wondered where the vomit receptacle was.

Dizzy with pain, she pushed the button for help. She pulled the sheet and blanket up over her torso. She gulped to ease the reflex to vomit. "Oh God, somebody help."

She closed her eyes and tried to think of something to sidetrack her panic. White bursting, throbbing images danced under her eyelids. She opened her eyes to search for the nurse call button again.

"How can I help… April, what's going on?"

Her nurse hurried to her side and held her wrist to check her pulse. She lowered the bed to its flat position. "Does that ease the pain a bit?"

"What?"

"I lowered the bed all the way. Does that ease the pain a bit?"

April gasped. "I'm dizzy, and my ears are ringing."

"Where is the pain?"

"It's in my neck now and in the back of my head."

"Okay, try to relax and rest. Don't move the bed, okay? I'll be right back."

April felt the pain in her shoulders and back subside, but she lay still, afraid to cause the agony to start all over again. *What if the bullet has moved? Could it cause more damage? What if I wouldn't ever walk again?*

"Okay, April. Are you still nauseated? What level of pain are you in?"

"I'm thirsty. I'm not as nauseous. The pain was a ten; now it's about a seven."

"Okay, I'm adding some pain medication to your IV. We'll give you some fluids, but I will only give you some ice chips to help you with your thirst. I don't want you to try to sit up."

"Okay."

"Can I turn the television on for you? This is hard now, but you need to lie flat for a bit."

"Okay, thanks. Can you tell me what happened?"

"I'm not sure. The doctor would be better to give you an answer to that. You were sitting up, right?"

April nodded her head. "I put the bed up and then pushed myself into a sitting position. I reached for my iPad, and then the pain started."

"Okay, I'll let the doctor know, but in the meantime, stay flat, and I'll get you some ice chips."

April felt tears slip down the side of her face and into her hair. "Okay."

***

"April?"

April was lying flat sleeping when Dr. Khumalo came in. She noticed April's lunch tray was untouched. She propped her laptop on the hospital table and scanned April's chart. Her mouth went to one side as she read, and her eyebrows knit. April stirred. Her eyes opened, and she looked at the doctor and smiled. The doctor's soft brown eyes and relaxed manner helped April feel friendly towards her. The doctor wore eyeliner, and her hair was in a messy bun at the base of her neck. To April, she was a younger doctor and reminded her of some of her teachers.

"Hi, April."

"Hi, Dr. Khumalo."

"Are you still feeling pain?"

"A little. It's a dull pain in my neck."

Dr. Khumalo arched her eyebrows to not give April the suggestion she was worried.

"You're not smiling," April said.

"No, I am not. I'm concerned."

She moved down to the foot of April's bed and uncovered her feet. April's foot didn't move as she ran her pen from the heel of her right foot to its toes. "April, are you normally ticklish?"

"Oh geez. The tech always laughs when I go for a pedicure because my foot jumps when she takes the calluses off."

"And what foot was that?"

"My left."

Dr. Khumalo ran her pen along the sole of her left foot. April's toes curled.

The doctor covered her feet again. Moving to her bedside so April could see her, Dr. Kumalo placed one hand on her chin and folded her other arm at her waist. April noticed her French manicure. "Tell me what you were doing when the pain started."

"The bed was kinda high, but I put my hands down and boosted myself up to a higher sitting position."

"And?"

"I moved to get my iPad."

"Did you twist at all?"

"Yes."

"That's when the pain started."

"It shot up my neck and into the back of my head."

"Have you sat up since then?"

"The nurse helped me sit up a little when my lunch came."

"I see. Why is your lunch still on the table?"

April shrugged

"Okay, I'll be back in a bit."

April searched around with her hands. Finding her phone, she brought it up to see the time. Only three. She placed her earbuds in her ears and touched Spotify to bring up her tunes. She could try one of the podcast stories.

Terry, the nurse on duty, walked in to check her vital signs. "The doctor told me we could bring your bed up."

She took the remote and pressed the button to move the head of the bed. April felt the bed move. Terry scanned her forehead for her temperature, then wrapped a blood pressure cuff around her arm. "Okay, are you comfortable?"

"I'm okay."

"Alright, good."

Terry took the tray from the table, even though April had not touched her lunch.

April busied herself looking for podcasts. Finding one, she lay back and closed her eyes.

Terry bustled back into her room. "April, you're running a bit of a temperature. Dr. Khumalo wants me to give you an antibiotic."

She sidled up to the intravenous pole and entered the medicine into the tubing. "She said she will see you again before she goes home tonight."

"Okay."

"Until then, rest." Terry put her hand on April's arm.

"Okay."

April had just finished the first episode of the podcast when Dr. Khumalo came in.

"Hi, April."

"Hi, Dr. Khumalo."

"How are you doing elevated a bit?"

"I'm okay but don't want to move around."

"Good. I agree. I'm concerned you have a fever."

"Why?"

"We talked about keeping an eye on your temperature, remember?"

"If it goes up, it may mean an infection."

"Correct. I ordered an antibiotic just in case. We will give it until tomorrow morning for your temperature to go down. You must eat. You didn't touch your lunch, and the nurse said you ate very little breakfast."

"I don't like Jello. I'm sick of chicken broth. The apple juice tastes like it was diluted."

"Okay. I need to keep you on a liquid diet."

"Why?"

"You need fluids."

Dr. Khumalo's eyes went from her computer to April. April's eyes welled up. "April, are you feeling pain?"

"No, not really. If I hadn't moved wrong…"

"No. No. I was ready to have you go home to rest, but you can't with a fever. I also want to run an EMG to determine nerve-to-muscle transition."

"My dad's a doctor. I kind of remember what that is."

"Okay, good. By the way, I'm going to order the catheter out. It may be causing irritation. The nurses can help you if you have to urinate. I'll see you tomorrow. I've told the nurse it's okay for you to raise the head of the bed to see the television or read, but don't raise it any higher.

April gave her a bit of a smile. "Good. Eat. I need you healthy."

***

Malaki sat and watched his daughter sleep. He wanted to reach out and touch her brown curls resting on her pale pink skin. She was small-boned and petite. At only five foot three, he and April's mom were worried when she wanted to play field hockey. But she was determined because she wanted to be with her friends, Madison and Ashley.

April woke to find her dad sitting next to her. He wore his lab coat, so she knew he had come from his research lab.

"Hey, how's the pain?"

April swallowed. "Better. Do you know what happened?"

Her dad stood. "Yes. Can I get you some water?"

"Yeah, I am so thirsty."

After he poured her water, her dad slipped his hand under her head and helped her guide the straw so she could drink.

"What did I do?"

"Nothing. You had a CSF leakage."

"Dad, English."

"You had what's called a Cerebrospinal Fluid leakage."

"Oh, I see." April laughed. "Actually, I don't."

Grinning, her dad said, "Okay, look. With your injury, as the swelling goes down, this happens. The pain is especially extreme because the fluid doesn't belong there."

"Will it happen again?"

"It could."

"Oh, geez."

"The doctors are talking about doing a test called Myelography. It's done by a radiologist to look for problems in the spinal canal. They'll have you lying down on a padded table, and you'll be drowsy and relaxed. You might have some aches and discomfort in your arms or legs afterward. Mom and I will be here when you return from the test."

"My legs, Dad?"

"Dr. Khumalo wants you to start physical therapy."

"Okay. Dr. Khumalo said my toes on my left foot moved today."

"She told me. That's good news."

Dr. Khumalo came by during her rounds the next day. "Hi, April. Your fever is down. That's a good sign."

"To start physical therapy?"

"Yes."

"To do the test?"

"Yes."

"To go home?"

"Not yet."

"What are you looking for?"

"I will look for how you are healing and placing of the bullet. If the bullet is causing the leak, I will remove it and place a blood patch over the wound. I hope it isn't, but from your reaction the other day, I am guessing it is."

"Will I be able to walk again, then?"

"With the partial you are experiencing, I am optimistic you will."

"How long will it take?"

"In some people, it takes weeks, sometimes eighteen months, sometimes years. But you are young and strong. I am cautiously optimistic."

April took a deep breath and bit her lower lip so she didn't start to cry. "Will I be able to go to prom or graduation?"

"April, let's just take one day at a time. Those are good goals, but let's take everything step by step. How are your studies going?"

9

April

The room was freezing. April woke and pulled the sheet and thin blanket around her shoulders. She was shaking she was so cold. When she didn't feel warmer after a few minutes, she pressed the nurse's station. "Hi, April. What can I do for you?" Said the night nurse.

"I'm really cold."

"I'll get you an extra blanket."

When the night nurse returned, she added the blanket for April. "Since I'm already here and you're awake, I thought I'd take your vitals."

The nurse went through the routine of checking April's blood pressure and checking her IVs and medication bags. She turned to April and pointed the thermometer at April's forehead.

"Hm, I'll be right back."

"Is there something wrong?" April asked.

"Your fever is back up and I'm going to check with the doctor about your medication. Don't worry, April."

April laid her head back and felt the warmth of the added blanket start to warm her body. She had just started to doze when the night nurse returned. In the haze of sleepiness, April felt the movement of air as the nurse moved close to her to change a medicine bag. She heard the rustling of her IV being checked and the interchange at the injection port.

***

"April, honey?"

April woke to see her mom standing next to her. "How do you feel?"

It took a second for April to notice she had a bit of a headache. She felt weak. "I don't feel really good."

Adele watched her daughter assess how she was feeling. April looked pale against the white pillowcase. "Are you warm enough?"

"Yes, but I have a headache and feel achy."

"The nurse said you had a fever last night so they changed your medication. The doctor should be doing her rounds soon, so we'll know more. Rest. I'll just sit with you and read."

"Okay."

***

April woke as an orderly brought her breakfast tray. She pushed the button to elevate the bed enough for her to eat. Her mom came in bringing flowers. "I thought your room needed a bit of brightening."

"Thanks, Mom. They're pretty."

"I brought some cards. I thought I could break up some of the monotony today."

"Don't you have any clients today?"

"I cancelled them. There wasn't anything urgent that couldn't wait until tomorrow."

The bustle outside her door alerted both April and her mom on the arrival of her doctor. There was a knock and the door opened as Dr. Khumalo said, "Hey, what's this I hear about you not feeling well today?"

"Yeah, I feel achy all over."

Dr. Khumalo paused as she looked at the laptop she carried with her. "Your fever is elevated again, April. This time it's 102."

The smile she had when she came into the room changed to a studious expression. She looked from her computer to April. "April, I'm going to have your urine tested for a UTI. I want to rule some things out before we even think this has anything to do with your injury. I'll give you some medication to make you comfortable. One thing you can do is rest." She nodded to the cards lying on April's table. "Looks like you have plans."

"We thought we'd play some cards to change up the activities today." Adele said.

"Good. But also get some rest. I'll change your diet to some light food to help you feel better too."

"Thank goodness! Mom, I don't think I'll eat chicken soup for a long time!"

"I can see the medication is already making you feel better," Dr. Khumalo said. "I'll be back once I get the test results. Probably late afternoon."

Adele and April nodded.

Dr. Khumalo turned and left her room. "After you eat your breakfast, we can play cards or you can nap," Adele said.

April pulled her breakfast tray closer to her and opened the lid of the cup. "Oh look, Mom, something different. Chicken broth."

***

"Good morning!"

Nurse Barbara always came in with a sunny disposition for her patients. When she saw April, she noted the sheets and blankets were pulled out from being tucked. "Hey, April. How are you?"

"I feel awful again. One minute I'm cold the next I am hot. I told the night nurse when she came in."

Barbara pulled up April's chart on her iPad. "It looks like your fever was up and down all night. Have you been drinking water?"

"Yes, but I think I'm out now."

As Barbara took April's blood pressure and temperature, she noted some bumps around April's nose. Her temperature was up again. "Okay, April. I'll make a note for Dr. Khumalo. She should be in early today."

After about fifteen minutes, Barbara came back into April's room. "April, the doctor asked me to take a sample from you. I have a swab and I'm going to take a sample from your nose, like the test for Covid."

She swabbed April's nose and then put the q-tip into a vial and closed the lid. "Dr. Khumalo asked this to have a rush on it for the lab. We should have the results soon."

April nodded and put her head back on the pillow. "Can I get you anything?" Barbara asked.

"No, just water. I think I'm going to sleep some more before I do homework."

"Geez, I'm sorry I forgot about your water."

April's eyes were closed when Barbara came back with the pitcher of water.

***

At noon, Dr. Khumalo and Malaki came into April's room at the same time. Malaki eyed his daughter who was attempting to read but looking drowsy. April's hair was curling around her pale face. Her eyes were showing dark circles. "Hi, honey. How are you feeling?"

"I'm ache all over, Dad. Hi, Dr. Khumalo."

"Hi, April. April, the test that was taken this morning showed you have MRSA."

"What's that?"

"It's a serious staph infection. It probably came about when they inserted the tube for urine. I've prescribed vancomycin, an antibiotic that should take care of it. Barbara will be right in to add it to your meds."

April nodded.

"You're eating?"

"I've had some oatmeal and toast."

"Good. I'll be back later to check on you."

April nodded again.

After the doctor left, April looked at her dad. "How can I get an infection when I'm in the hospital?"

Malaki sat in the chair next to April's bed. "It happens. Actually, it happens so often they call it HA-MRSA."

"Ha, MRSA. That's weird."

"I know. Staph is on the skin all the time. But when something is inserted into the body, it can occur. What we have to make sure right now is that it doesn't get into your blood stream. That's why Dr. Khumalo rushed the lab results."

"What happens if it gets into my blood stream."

"You could be seriously ill."

10

Ben

Marcie had spent the morning in meetings and prepping for the noon news. She paused to leave a note on the desk of Greg Stanton, the investigation reporter, at 10TV. They've been a team for three years and have complete control over what they cover within reason. At least, it's what their bosses always add when they discussed their proposals. She wanted him to join her in the control room as soon as he got into the station because one of the latest segments was the arraignment of Ben "Sonny" Franklin.

Sitting at the second tier of desks and broadcast equipment, she listened to the cacophony of voices preparing for the noon news. The row of monitors was set to logos, upcoming advertisements, shots of the anchors, and live shots, all poised to be cued. Someone viewing this room for the first time might feel the frenetic energy between the engineers and director, but for the personnel in the room, it's their lifeblood. The constant banter between the director, the producer, the sound engineers, the anchors, and the camera people would put an inexperienced ear on edge. A rush of adrenaline was always present when breaking news occurred. Today, it was the coverage of Franklin's arraignment.

Through the murmurs of the personnel and flashing monitors, Marcie concentrated on veteran news reporter Harriet Parkins outside the Hamilton County Courthouse. Luckily, the rain had stopped, so Harriet and her photographer, Seth Taylor, didn't have to work with an umbrella. Running her fingers through her hair as Harriet read her notes on her cell, she prepped for her live shot. Marcie knew they had spent the morning in Court Room number three.

Marcie looked up as Greg slid into the chair next to her. He was a bear of a man. He towered over most individuals at six foot five, but as Marcie found out, he was gentle unless someone crossed him. She pointed toward the monitors with the live shot cued up. "So, Franklin's arraignment?"

Marcie nodded as the familiar jingle started the noon news. Dave Sweeney and Killian Gregory were at the anchor desk. Killian placed her mirror and lip gloss under the desk as Director Joe Friedman called for camera one.

"Good afternoon. I'm Dave Sweeney with Killian Gregory. Benjamin (Sonny) Franklin was arraigned in Hamilton County Common Pleas Court this morning. Harriet Parkins has the story."

"Cut to Harriet," said Joe.

"Benjamin (Sonny) Franklin was arraigned in Hamilton County Common Pleas Court this morning on three counts of felonious assault. If you remember, Franklin shot at three Springridge High School seniors back in October. April Simmons was wounded and remains at Midtown Medical Center."

"Cut to video of the proceedings," Joe said.

The paneled courtroom appeared on the screen with a shot of Ben Franklin in the foreground.

Facing the judge's bench, his eyes kept shifting side to side and back to the judge. He was wearing the orange jumpsuit with FC on the back. His young court-appointed lawyer, Stewart Joseph, stood by him dressed in a pinstriped suit, white shirt, and red tie. The audience could hear the rustle of papers and people shifting in their chairs.

The camera switched to a shot with Judge Arthur Radcliffe on the bench. With his reading glasses balanced on his nose, the judge turned to the defendant's side of the room. "Benjamin Franklin, you have been accused of three counts of felonious assault. How do you plea?"

"Guilty."

"Speak up, Mr. Franklin."

"Guilty."

"Do you have anything to say?"

"Judge, these kids have been knocking on my doors and windows for years. They threw eggs and manure at my house. I didn't have my lights on for Halloween. They were trespassing on my property."

"What time is Trick or Treat over in Springridge?"

"Six to eight o'clock."

"What time were the three girls on your property?"

"Closer to midnight. I needed to go to work the next morning."

"The curfew in Springridge is ten o'clock, your honor," said his attorney.

The judge nodded and wrote a note. "Did you call the police?"

"This time?"

"Yes, this time, Mr. Franklin."

"No, my mom called the police before, and nothing happened."

"No police report was recorded at the Springridge Police Department." Prosecutor Edward Jackson's voice could be heard.

"When was the last time you filed a police report, Mr. Franklin?"

"Years ago. My mother was still alive."

Judge Radcliffe seemed to study Ben and then returned to his notepad.

"I didn't mean to hurt anybody. The kids kept coming to my property, and I had to protect it."

"The young lady you shot is still in the hospital. Do you feel any remorse for shooting her?"

"Judge, the three girls knocked on my door. They looked like they were going to come back when I shot my gun."

His attorney's head snapped to look at this client. His mouth moved as if to shush him.

"Cut to live shot. Three, two, one."

The live shot of Harriet Perkins returned to the screen. "Benjamin Franklin received fifteen years in prison by Judge Arthur Radcliffe, the maximum sentence."

"Cut to Camera One. Three, two, one."

Dave Sweeney returned to the screen to cut to a commercial.

Marcie nudged Greg to leave the control room. "Well, that's short and sweet," Greg said.

"Yes, it was."

They stopped in the break room to grab some coffee. "You still think there's something wrong? What bothers you about this? The guy shot a girl, no expression of remorse, and he seemed defiant."

"I agree. But didn't the original story say this happened continuously? A senior prank?"

"Yeah, I think so. So?"

"Shouldn't he or his attorney comment about that to the judge?"

"Maybe, but I don't think it would've changed the result. He pled guilty."

"He did. But should he have?"

"His lawyer would have discussed that with him."

"Yes, he should have, but did he? Could you look into this? What was his name, Joseph Stewart?"

"I think it was the other way around."

"Okay, Stewart Joseph. My instincts say there's a story beyond what we just saw."

11

April

Two more weeks passed before April started feeling better. It took about three days for the antibiotic to take effect and a few more days before April had the motivation to work on anything for school. She kept falling asleep when she tried to read.

April was engrossed in a video about Prussia assigned by her IB Euro teacher but was interrupted by a knock. A woman came pushing a wheelchair with a board on its armrests. April closed her laptop. "Hello?"

"Hi, April. I'm Connie, your OT. Your occupation therapist."

"Hi, Connie."

"I'm here to teach you how to get into your wheelchair from your bed."

"Oh, wow."

Connie came over to her bed and moved it to the lowest setting. She brought the wheelchair over and collapsed the arm closest to the bed. While she did this, April watched.

"Um, Connie. I can't move my legs."

"I know that. April, I'll take care of you." Connie's eyes smiled as she said this.

"What if I fall?"

"You won't. It will be fine." She lined the board up, bridging the bed and wheelchair. "Okay, April, do you remember how you slid across the bleachers in the gym?"

April nodded. "That's what I want you to do today. Slide over onto the board. You look pretty strong, and I'll be here to help."

April, nervous, looked at the board. "The last time I tried anything like this, twisting or moving, I got a CSF."

Connie nodded. "Dr. Khumalo told me you might be concerned. But she thinks you're ready for this. Put your hands under your torso and scoot over onto the board."

April put her hands under her and pushed down on the bed. Connie moved her tray and computer out of the way. April shifted to avoid twisting her body, dragging her legs. Connie smiled. "Good April. I'll move your legs for you this time. But soon, I'll ask you to move them yourself."

She placed her hands under April's calves and slipped them to dangle. "Now, April, move over to the chair."

The move took several minutes, but she looked up at Connie, smiling. "I did it."

"Great. Looks like you have two more visitors."

April saw two smiling individuals standing by the door of her room. The man was about five eleven, average build, and lean. The woman with him had dark brown hair styled in a low ponytail, porcelain skin, and large dark eyes. She was of average height and small-boned. They both were wearing gold shirts with an insignia of some sort and khaki pants.

"Hi."

"Hi. April. I'm Eric, and this is Tessa. We're going to do a bit of physical therapy today."

"Okay."

"How about we take you where we work?"

"How are you going to do that?"

Eric looked at Tessa. "Well, I guess we can't expect her to know how to get there."

Tessa smiled and shook her head. "I suppose we can't. I've brought you another hospital gown," she said.

April smiled. "Tessa, I have a robe in the closet over there. Would that work?"

Tessa had unfurled a hospital gown with some finesse but smiled back. "Better yet!"

Tessa took a plush purple robe from the closet and brought it to April. She helped April put it on by sliding it behind her, and both Eric and Tessa helped her slip her arms into it. Tessa tucked April's robe around her. "And we are out of here!" Eric said.

Connie walked out with them. "You guys are spoiling her. Next time I see you, April, I will teach you how to operate the wheelchair. We will practice so you can handle different obstacles."

"Thanks, Connie," April said.

After taking an elevator to the first floor, the three passed through a series of hallways. April was just happy to get out of her room.

They toured her through where she would do physical therapy. There were rooms containing high and low tables and mats in rows. Individual rooms were marked with colors, with a single table and set of waist-high parallel bars. Multi-colored bands were hanging everywhere. Patients were exercising on bikes and apparatus. Patients with walkers slowly made their way down hallways accompanied by a physical therapist shadowed by another therapist with a wheelchair. Many patients wore tan belts that physical therapists clutched as they walked with them. Tessa also said there was a pool area with underwater treadmills that assisted people learning to walk again.

Tessa took her back to her room after her tour. Terry, the nurse on duty, helped April to the bathroom, and then Tessa and she assisted April back into bed. Tessa massaged both her legs, feet, and ankles. She manipulated her legs, explaining she wanted to get blood flowing into April's muscles and lubricate her joints. Tessa stated she or Eric would be back daily until April went home. From there, April would be an outpatient and coming to the facility.

After Tessa left, April tried to return to her studies. She felt a lump form in her throat, and tears ran down her face when she realized this was the first sign she would walk again.

During the next week, Tessa or Eric had her down at the facility. They had her work with light weights to strengthen her upper body. "Tessa," said April, "we always worked with the machines at school."

"What weight did you lift?"

"Twenty-five to thirty-five pounds."

"That's good, April. But you last trained a month ago. We

need to get your upper body strength up again because you will be lifting yourself out of the wheelchair or pulling yourself to go on the mat for therapy. Don't you hate having someone help you onto the toilet?"

April blushed. "Yes."

"Well, Connie will show you how to do that again yourself."

The next day, Connie came in pushing a wheelchair with a board balanced over its armrests. April was working on a math problem. She had tried several times to work with a formula and could not find one part of the equation. "Hi April, we're going to work on mobility in the wheelchair today."

Tossing the math book on the bed next to her, April said, "Good. I need a break from that, anyway. How are you in trig?"

Connie laughed. "I am definitely not one to ask."

She pushed the wheelchair to the side of the bed and reached for the remote to lower April's bed. "Do you have a robe to wear?"

"Yes, it's in the closet."

"Good. While I get your robe, why don't you start finding your way to the wheelchair.

"Okay."

April uncovered her legs and pushed herself up onto the board. She paused as Connie helped her put on her robe, then she waited.

"Go ahead and finish, April."

April hesitated. "Aren't you going to help me with my legs?"

"Not this time. I'm going to get behind you to balance you as you cross over to the chair."

April watched as Connie moved to go behind her. "But how?"

"You're a smart girl, April. You can do it."

April sat for a minute. She leaned toward the bed and physically moved her right leg over the side of the bed. She looked at Connie. Connie nodded and smiled. April leaned to right and held the edge of the board with her right hand and with her left hand, moved her left leg, but she hadn't moved on the board enough to have room for her leg to dangle. Connie placed her hands on April's hips. "Go ahead, move over a bit more."

April hesitated. She slowly moved herself over a bit more, inching centimeters. Leaning to move her body, she pitched forward. Connie held her in place. "You are doing well, April. Scoot back a bit more on the board. It will help you feel more secure."

April scooted back, which allowed her left leg to fall. "You'll get better at judging, April."

April nodded. She pressed her lips together as she continued to place her hands down on the board and move her weight to the chair. When she reached for the armrest of the chair, she maneuvered too far and almost fell onto the seat of the chair. Connie caught her as she fell and righted her. "Take it slow, April. You'll get there."

April smiled when she centered herself in the chair. "I will help today with removing the board from under you. Tomorrow, you will do it yourself."

April nodded.

***

Dr. Khumalo said she was releasing her to go home three weeks later. She was to return as an outpatient to do physical therapy three times a week. Her dad inquired whether they should have a physical therapist come to the house when April was not going to PT at MSU. Dr. Khumalo said they could if they chose.

A Welcome Home sign decorated the front porch of their house. As her parents helped her from the car into her wheelchair, she heard, "Surprise!" Friends from her IB classes and her Field Hockey team had jumped out from behind the Welcome Home sign. They hugged her as her dad pushed her up the ramp that covered the front steps. They all followed her into the house, where they turned on music, danced, and ate the food her mom had for them. After two hours, the kids left. Ashley later told April her mom and dad had encouraged her to let kids know April was tired.

Thirty minutes later, her parents had cleaned up the banquet of treats and were sitting in the family room watching the news. They noticed April was nodding off in her chair. Her dad sat on the chair beside her and said, "April, we have one more surprise for you."

He pushed her chair to her mother's office. The doorknob had been changed to a handle. "Go ahead, open it," her dad said.

April opened the door to find her upstairs bedroom had been moved. The walls had been repainted to pale lavender, and her decorations, furniture, books, and trophies were all in place. "Dad! Mom! Thank you! This is so cool."

"The only thing we could not do was move all your clothes into the closet down here. So now they're in the small closet and the hall closet."

"We added a vanity so you could put on your makeup, and you will use the guest bathroom. Your dad had a bench installed in the shower."

"I can't believe you did this!"

"We thought this would be easier for you."

"Did you move your office to my room upstairs?"

"Well, yes."

April wasn't sure why this bothered her. Could it mean her parents didn't believe she would walk again?

12

Marcie and Greg

"What exactly do you think you can accomplish?" Kim Wolford asked. She held the position of WCMS Executive News producer/Community Relations Director and served as Marcie and Greg's direct boss.

Since Kim hated sitting behind a desk while reporters, producers, and photographers developed story ideas, they sat in a small conference room. They decided this was the best place to reason out story ideas. Kim placed a tablet in front of her to jot down notes. Marcie Reynolds had progressed from Writer/Researcher to Morning and Special Investigative Producer after a long hiatus as a political wife and mother. Greg Stanton, an award-winning WCMS Investigative Reporter, handled a long list of investigations viewers phoned in. The viewing area for the station covered Central and parts of Southern Ohio. The three decided if Greg should take on a story or if one of the other reporters needed to cover an item. Kim was still amazed at how the partnership of Marcie and Greg began. Kim had to warn Greg often not to give Marcie a hard time, and now Marcie and Greg finished each other's sentences.

"We need to do more research on the principles of the story. Why did the girls go to this house? How could a prank center on a person's home? We need more about the guy who owned the house, and why did he shoot at the girls? It's a small town.

Why not just find out the identity of the kids and call their parents? Or the police?"

"I can tell this has been on your mind, Marcie."

"It's bothered her since this happened," Greg said. "But I have questions too. From what I understand, Springridge is a close community. The video of the house showed the yard to be overgrown. Why wasn't he cited? The reports said he worked at the library. He wasn't some…"

"I believe you said nutcase," Marcie said.

"Yeah, well. For want of a better word."

"If this was a senior prank, I'd like to know if the parents knew and why they didn't stop the bullying before it came to this? We've run stories about the dangers of bullying. Here we have one close-up." Kim said.

"It looks like harassment."

"What's the difference?"

"What if it's both?" Marcie asked. "I looked up both definitions. Bullying is when someone uses aggression to intimidate or degrade someone. Harassment is when the behavior of bullying is directed at someone, and it's based on a protected class of people."

"So, why this guy?" Greg asked.

"Did you check with Harriet, who covered the story?"

"She told me it was pretty cut and dry. She heard Franklin ask his attorney if the girls would be charged with trespassing, and the attorney ignored him. We looked at the tape. His tone and body language expressed showed anger when he answered questions posed by the judge. He showed no remorse."

"Court-appointed attorney?"

"Real young."

"I would like to check on how April, the girl, is doing. Maybe we could get a feel for the town. She would be a good story if she was courageous and walked again," Marcie said.

Kim raised her eyebrows. "That would be inspirational. Okay, you two. Let's see where this takes you. Keep me posted as you investigate this. If you don't have anything in, say, two or three weeks, let's let it go."

As Marcie and Greg walked down the stairs to their desks, Greg said, "That was a good idea to mention the story idea. Did it just come to you?"

Marcie smiled. "Yep."

"Got time to decide how we are going to proceed?"

"Yes."

"Good, it's two o'clock, and I'm starved. Lunch?"

13

Ben

Ben underwent transfer and processing into the Madison Correctional Facility. The indignity of the initial examination brought him close to tears. He told the examiner he had allergies. The guard snorted. "You won't have any allergies in here."

The prison uniform proved to be uncomfortable. Ben liked the crispness of his ironed shirts and the softness of his khaki pants. The uniform was baggy and rough. He also had a preference for underwear that had a soft and tight feel. These were neither.

The guard then led him and eight new prisoners through the locked doors. Ben kept his head down and looked at everything side-eyed. The guard showed them classrooms and the recreation center where, in the evening, inmates played ping-pong and watched television. Ben looked up when the guard herded the group to the library. At least one place he would find familiarity. It disappointed him. The shelves held a few books, with some propped up by small stacks. In the middle of the room was one table with two chairs. The guard said as they stood in the hall, they would meet with a counselor who would talk to them about where they could fit into the community and would recommend classes. They'd also be assigned responsibilities, such as laundry, helping custodians, or garbage detail.

The guard bragged about the prison, stating that it held the title of being Ohio's smallest and best facility. Since all the men were new inmates, nobody could respond.

He informed them that new prisoners were assigned older inmates to assist them in adapting to the facility. From his clipboard, the guard read that Ben had been matched with Rick Fleming. The guard said they would meet their mentors later in the day. Now, they would continue to their assigned cells.

One by one, the men were left in their cells. Each cell had two bunks. Each man had a place for his things under his bunk. They also had a single desk drawer where they could place items. The guard informed them that the prison guards had the authority to inspect the designated areas and seize anything they deemed unsafe.

Ben was the fifth person to be shown his cell. The guard who had the name Paul on his uniform mentioned to him that his cellmate's name was Brody Mercury. Ben was then left on his own.

He must have stood, not moving, for a half hour, staring at the vacant bunk. A folded bottom sheet, a pillow, a pillowcase, and a dark green blanket rested on the mattress. Nothing looked comfortable.

He sensed someone enter his cell. "Hi. Um, I guess you're my new cellmate?"

Both men stood still for a moment. "Um. I'm Brody. Um, could you turn around and introduce yourself or move so I can get around you?

He didn't make eye contact with Brody when he turned around. "My name is Ben."

"Okay, that's a start." Brody stuck out his hand.

Ben saw Brody's depigmented right hand. He shook Brody's hand and looked up at his face. "You have vitiligo."

"No kidding! Wow. You're a smart one." Brody slipped by him.

"A kid came into the library once, and I looked it up. It's caused by an autoimmune condition."

"Yup. So, you looked it up."

Ben looked down again. "Yes."

Both stood silent for an extra minute. Brody then lay on his bunk and covered his eyes with his arm. Ben looked at the desk chair, pulled it out, and sat.

***

Rick Fleming paused on the outside of Ben and Brody's cell. Ben sat at the desk with his hands folded in front of him. Brody lay on his bunk. "Ahem."

No movement. "Well, I'm not one for manners, but clearly, someone is standing out in front of your cell."

Ben turned and looked at him. Rick stood about Ben's height with a medium build. He had short, dark blonde hair, and his chin sported whitish-blonde bristles. Brody lifted his head. "Hi, Brody. How are ya?"

Brody swung his legs around. "Fine, Rick. This one doesn't talk much." He stood. "See ya in the cafeteria."

Rick nodded. "Well, I don't mind someone who doesn't talk much. I can fill in the gaps pretty easily. Think you can eat something yet?"

Ben stood and walked out of his cell. "You're lucky you got to be with Brody. He's an okay guy. A little touchy about his skin, but friendly, not nosy. You get him on the Bengals or the Reds, and he will go on forever. Do you like sports, Ben?"

"I'm not into them much."

"Not even The Midtown State? You came from near Columbus, so I figured you might be into one of them."

Ben shook his head.

"You graduated from Columbus State. What did you study?"

"IT."

"Were you working when you got into trouble?"

"I worked at the library in town."

"Using your IT degree? That's good. I'll pass that along to your counselor. He might have an idea for you to use it here."

"That would be nice of you."

"Okay, here we are at the cafeteria. It works just like your high school cafeteria. There aren't a lot of choices, but the gal who runs the place tries to fit everyone's needs here."

"I like vegetables. I stay away from red meat."

"We have chicken a lot because it costs less, they tell me. You should be good."

Ben took a tray and slid it along. Someone let out a howl, and they heard a crash. A rush of running feet. Next came shouts and a chorus of loud, low voices. Almost simultaneously, "Okay, men, let's get back to your dinners." The sound of double doors opening and closing.

Rick noted Ben's reaction. His job would be to prevent him from running to see what was happening. But Ben had turned toward the sounds with his tray and food choices and froze. His wide eyes and raised eyebrows reminded Rick of an animal getting ready to run away from danger. "Ben, it's okay. Whatever went on, the guards took care of it."

He put his hand on Ben's shoulder. Ben moved from under his hand but stayed in the same place.

Rick tried again. "What would you like to drink?"

Continuing to face toward the sounds, Ben said, "Water."

Rick urged him on by gesturing with his tray. "Okay, let's get you some by the soda machine right over there."

They exited the food selection area to the vast cafeteria. "Hey Ben, it looks like there are two seats where Brody is. Let's go."

Ben followed and sat. Rick nodded to Brody. "Ben, this here is Chee, Tracy and Ken. Brody hangs with them."

Ben put his hands in his lap. He nodded at the men. Tracy and Ken looked at Brody. Tilting his head to the side, Chee kept his eyes on Ben. Brody raised his eyebrows and shrugged his shoulders. Ben picked up his fork and ate. Rick noticed how Ben kept his food separate on his plate. He thought he'd better ask the counselor about Ben being quiet and his reactions.

After dinner, they walked to the recreation center. "Ben, do you have a favorite show you follow every week?"

"No. I don't watch much television. I only like old movies like Spartacus, North by Northwest, and The Maltese Falcon. Could we go to the library, Rick?"

Rick glanced at the clock. It may be open for another hour. Let's go."

They had to go over to the administration section of the building. "What type of books do you like?"

"Anything I'm curious about. I read about the autoimmune situation like Brody has."

"You have?"

"I've read about climate change and wind and solar energy. And old movies."

"Wow, that's something. Well, let's see if there is anything in here you would be curious about."

  ` Rick opened the door for Ben. He nodded to the inmate, who checked in books. Rick picked up a book about bipolar disorders and looked at the cover. Terry Blackman, the counselor, had schooled him about this when his former wife came to visit him. Concerned one of his kids might be bipolar, she wanted to discuss what to do. He didn't sleep well and was being belligerent. It turned out he was just being a difficult adolescent. Rick turned abruptly, aware of someone behind him. "My mother was bipolar," Ben said.

Recovering, Rick said, "Hm, she was?"

Ben said yes and walked away to examine another stack of books.

After Ben had looked around and checked out the book about bipolar disorder, they headed back to Ben's cell. "Thursday, after you have some time to adjust, I'll be back to take you to breakfast, and then we'll walk down for your appointment with Terry Blackman, your counselor."

"Why am I seeing a counselor?"

"He wants to meet you, and you'll talk about if there are any classes you might like to take here."

"Okay."

Brody hadn't returned to their cell, so Ben sat at the desk and read his book.

"The doors lock and lights out at 11, Ben," said Rick.

"Okay."

14

April

April was sitting in her wheelchair, waiting for an appointment with Dr. Khumalo. Her dad had gone to the restroom. She was hoping the doctor would tell her she could go to school as soon as the holiday break was over. Despite social media, she couldn't help but feel claustrophobic at home with just a caregiver and her tutor, even though she tried not to complain. She would roll from room to room, needing to move into a different space. The weather reflected her mood with low clouds and storms. She wondered what was happening in her classes and if she would have difficulty catching up.

The nurse opened the waiting room door. "April?"

April said yes and pushed her wheels forward.

"Hey, let me help."

"No. No, let me do it myself. I'm good." April said.

It was important to her to do things for herself. She felt less helpless and more independent. Her dad had encouraged her. Her mom worried, but relented after about a week.

After the nurse did the preliminary checks, the doctor came in. Dr. Khumalo sat and read her chart, which contained last week's progress with Eric and Tessa, her physical therapists.

"Well, it says you regained some sensation on your left side."

The doctor checked her reflexes on her left leg. April felt the tap, but her leg didn't respond. She couldn't feel the tap on her right leg, and it did not respond. "How are you getting around at your house?"

"I manage as much as I can. Dad has installed some bars and things."

"Are you going outside at all?"

"I've gone down a couple of driveways when the weather is okay. I'm so glad it hasn't snowed."

"Okay, that's good."

Dr. Khumalo stood and went to the door. "Nurse, would you invite April's father in? His name is Dr. Simmons." To April, she said, "I am concerned there has been no progress in your right leg."

April's dad came into the exam room. "Dr. Simmons, hello. I was just telling April I'm concerned she was not progressing as I hoped. The swelling should be down enough for her to have some feeling on her right side and even more in her left leg. The EMG is still showing some interruption with the nerves in her L1 area."

"What are you thinking, doctor?"

April sat listening to the doctor. She realized she was holding her breath.

Dr. Khumalo said, "April, there isn't really any timetable for an incomplete spinal injury. Every spinal injury is different, and every patient experiences different outcomes. However, the largest spike of recovery occurs in the first three to six months post- injury. I believe we need to remove the bullet."

April's eyes teared as she tried to focus on her dad. "It's only been three months. I haven't had any CS —." She looked at her dad.

"CSF leakages."

"And I've been trying…"

"She knows you have April." Her dad came over to hug her. "But honey, the bullet must be pressing on your nerves."

"But I've missed half my senior year. Will the operation stop me from returning to school next semester? Will I be able to walk?"

Her dad lifted her chin and handed her a tissue to wipe her eyes and nose. "Do you remember we will take it one day at a time? I know this is hard."

They both focused on Dr. Khumalo. She had her lips pressed hard together. "I don't think so. These situations vary from person to person. You are young and an athlete, which is why you've gotten this far. I just can't guarantee anything until we see how you do. I suspect you will still be in your chair, but we will see."

She turned to April's father. "Our assistant will check the hospital and see when we can schedule the procedure. Until then, we will continue the physical therapy with Eric and Tessa. April, we need to work to make sure your muscles don't lose their tone."

"Can we wait until after Christmas?" April said. Her voice was soft and tearful.

"It's very close, isn't it?" Said Dr. Khumalo. "Do you shop online? At least you won't experience the crowded stores."

April bit her lower lip. She knew the doctor was trying to be kind and positive, but she was fighting to not be resentful and miserable.

15

Marcie and Greg

Marcie sat at her desk, daydreaming. Killian came off the set after the morning news to grab some coffee. "Hey, you look a million miles away."

"Well, maybe not that far away. Do you remember the girl shot in Springridge months ago?"

Killian leaned against Marcie's desk and sipped her coffee. "I do. Didn't the guy who shot her go to prison?"

"Yes, he did. I was wondering how she was doing. If I remember right, she was paralyzed."

Killian shrugged her shoulders. "Call her. I'd like to know that, too."

Marcie wrote herself a note and turned to her computer.

***

After a long 9:30 production meeting, Marcie went to her desk and returned several calls then sat back to take a break. Because of one call, Marcie needed to follow up with Greg, but he was away from his desk. She picked up her phone and called the Simmons's home phone number.

"Hello, Simmons's residence."

"Mrs. Simmons. This is Marcie Reynolds from 10TV. I just wanted to call and ask how April was doing."

"Are you a reporter?"

"No, I'm a producer here at the station. Really. I wanted to know how she was."

"That's nice of you. Um. Well, she is better. She will undergo surgery to remove the bullet in a few weeks. The doctor didn't feel she was progressing as well as she could. The bullet is pressing on some nerves, causing her right side not to respond to therapy. She has a way to go."

"Does she have feeling on her left side?"

"Yes, she is regaining some strength there. Her physical therapists have been wonderful. They work her hard. She gets frustrated. But I think she is doing better."

"May I speak with her?"

"She's at therapy now. If she isn't too tired, why don't I have her call you?"

"I would like that. Let me give you my number where I can be reached here at the station."

***

Marcie was leaving for the day when her phone buzzed. Marcie sighed. She was expecting a dozen calls, so she retraced her steps.

"Hello, this is Marcie Reynolds."

"Ms. Reynolds, this is April Simmons."

"April, I'm glad you caught me. I was just leaving."

"Oh, I'm sorry."

"No, that's okay. I told your mom I wanted to know how you are doing."

"I'm okay."

"Your mom mentioned you are scheduled for surgery."

"Yes. The doctor didn't like how I was progressing, so they decided to take the bullet out."

"That's rough. Have you been able to return to school?"

"No. I've had a tutor. I've managed to keep up for the most part."

"Well, that's good. You'll graduate on time?"

"Yes. I've been accepted into two universities."

"Congratulations. Which ones?"

"Miami of Ohio and The Midtown State University."

"So, which are you leaning toward?"

There was silence on the other end of the phone. "April?"

"Well, my friends and I planned to go to Miami. We hoped to play Field Hockey there."

"Oh, I see."

"Yeah."

"Well, what do you and your parents think now?"

"We're waiting to make any decisions. I would like to get back to school and see my friends."

"I'll bet. April, is your mom home?"

"Yes, she has rearranged her schedule, so when I go to therapy, she picks me up and then works from home."

"That's good."

"Yeah, she'll do that until I can get around easier. I'll get her."

"Hello?"

"Hi, Mrs. Simmons. April sounds a little down."

"Hi, Ms. Reynolds. Call me Adele."

"Only if you call me Marcie. I would like to send her some Channel 10 swag if that would cheer her a bit. We have hats, tee shirts, whatever I can put my hands on."

"Marcie, that would be nice. Hold on a second." Marcie heard her open a sliding glass door and then close it. "She has been disappointed her friends haven't visited more often. I blame myself because I wouldn't let them visit when this first happened. Now, I realize how much she needs them."

"I raised two of them. Teens get distracted. Let me see what I can find, and maybe that will cheer her up. Give her something to tell them to come and see."

"Thank you. That would be great."

When Adele returned inside, April asked her mom what Marcie said. "Oh, she wants to arrange a little surprise for you. You'll see."

16

Ben

After two days, Brody said, "Come on, man. It's time you take a shower."

Ben had taken care to take sponge baths but avoided the community showers.

"Look, we all have assigned times. Mine is the same as yours because it's our section on the floor. Now, come on. It's cool."

Ben mimicked Brody. He took his underwear and a clean uniform, his prison clothes sack with his prison number stenciled, and wore flip-flops. They were given towels in the shower area. His eyes were on the floor or looking at the wall as he undressed. He hung his clothes sack on a hook and placed his used uniform and underwear in the sack. The towel was wrapped tightly around his waist. He wasn't sure what to do with the towel when he walked toward the shower room. When they reached the showers, Brody motioned for him to place it next to his towel on hooks outside the shower room.

The thick steam of the showers gave Ben a sense of modesty. He found a spigot that had a strong spray of water. The soap canister hung next to the spigot. Following Brody's advice, he quickly soaped his hair and body, keeping his face dry and his eyes clear. He heard a bodiless voice as he rinsed. "If it ain't Pinto and his new roommate."

"Ignore him." He heard Brody say. "Let's go."

"Hey, ya sure you rinsed thoroughly?"

Emerging from the steam, Ben saw a tall, solid, human shape walking toward them. Ben wrapped his arms around himself, tapping his right hand on his left arm, backed against

62

the wall, and squeezed his eyes shut. "Ben, come on. We're leaving the showers. Come on, man."

Ben felt a hand grab his arm. Brody, in his rush to leave, slipped but caught himself before he fell.

"Here." Brody handed Ben his towel. "You can grab another one over here."

Ben automatically wrapped the towel around his waist. He kept looking over his shoulder as they rushed to where they had left their clothes sacks. "Who, who was that?"

"Keno. His cell is at the far corner of our block. What was that all about in there? I told you to not close your eyes, man. You got to be aware of your surroundings in here."

"He called you Pinto."

"Yeah."

"That's wrong."

Ben and Brody were still damp but were putting on their clothes. "Yeah. But who's going to stop him? I ignore him when I can."

"When you can?"

"We'll talk about it later. Dry your hair. It'll take a while to dry in here."

***

Late morning, Ben was to meet Dr. Terry Blackwell. Rick met him for breakfast and walked him to Terry's office to introduce them. Terry was in the administrative office area near the library.

His office was like someone's den. He had insisted twenty years ago that his office could not be sterile. It had to feel safe. He had it painted white with a warm yellow tone. Bookshelves loaded with books (no knick knacks in a prison) and modern paintings with warm colors graced the walls. He had a desk and file cabinets (painted warm colors) and two comfortable honey-brown chairs in front of the desk. When prisoners were in the room, nothing was on the desk. No personal pictures, folders, nothing. His office had two windows, but there were no blinds or drapes.

Rick knocked on the door. "Enter."

Terry walked to them as they came through the threshold.

"Rick, it's good to see you. Ben, it's nice to meet you."

Ben nodded and looked down. He was concentrating on the color of the floor.

"How are things going, Rick?"

"Ben is doing fine. He had a visit to the library when he first arrived."

"I saw he worked in a library before he came here."

"You saw he had an IT degree?"

"I did."

"Brody and him are getting along, I think."

Ben nodded.

"Brody's a good man. Okay, Rick, we'll take it from here.

Rick nodded and left.

"Ben, why don't you sit and we can talk?"

Ben put his hand through his hair. He walked to the chairs but hesitated where to sit. "Whichever one makes you comfortable, Ben."

Ben sat with his back to Terry. Terry walked over and sat in the opposite chair.

"How are you doing with Rick?"

Ben looked up for the first time. He looked at Terry and saw a friendly but formidable man. His eyes were piercing. His face was chiseled, and he had no hair on his head. "I'm doing okay."

"And with Brody?"

"A man called him Pinto today."

The right eyebrow raised on Terry's face. "And what did Brody do?"

"He told me to ignore him, and we got out of the showers."

Terry nodded. "Good. Tell me about yourself."

"I like old movies like Spartacus, North by Northwest, and The Maltese Falcon. I want to climb Mt. Rushmore like Cary Grant."

"Ben, how can I help you?"

Ben shrugged.

Terry observed Ben as he talked. "Ben, have you been diagnosed with autism?"

"Yes. But I'm highly functional."

"When were you diagnosed?"

"When I was a kid."

"Do you have any idea what that means?"

"It's a bio-neurological developmental disability. It's a social and communicative disorder. I've read about it."

"Okay, good. What does that mean to you?"

Looking down and not meeting Terry's eyes, Ben said, "I have trouble talking to people sometimes."

"And?"

"I don't like meat because it's hard to digest."

"Rick told me you like to keep your foods separate."

Ben nodded.

"Where would you like to work here at Madison?"

"I'm good at computers. I like the library."

"We have a desk clerk already in the library, but I'll check with the warden's office. We talked about expanding the much needed library services. I would like to enroll you in our Library Services program. You can also take courses online and get credit from Ashland University."

"Okay."

"What's your assignment here?"

"The guard told me I could help with custodial duties now, and in the spring, I can work in the garden."

"Okay. Let me check in with you again next week. Think about what I've said."

"Okay."

Rick was waiting when Ben opened the door to Terry's office to leave. "Turns out a visitor is waiting for you, so I'll walk you down to that area, and then we'll talk about your visit with Terry."

"Okay."

Rick walked him through another series of hallways and opened the door to a large room with tables and chairs. A guard took his name and number. "Your attorney wants to talk to you," he said.

"Ben, I'll be outside in the hall," Rick said.

Ben walked over to where Stewart Joseph sat with papers on the table. Ben stood behind the chair opposite Stewart. Stewart pushed back the chair and stood.

Offering Ben his hand, he said, "Hi, Ben. Remember me, I'm your lawyer, Stewart Joseph."

Ben shook his hand and nodded. He sat down. Stewart looked around, tucked his tie, and also sat. Stewart scooted his chair forward. "Ben, the court notified me that you must pay restitution costs."

"What does that mean?"

"Your…ahem…victim has been in the hospital and will need extensive physical therapy since you…ahem…shot her."

"Did they pay a fine for trespassing?"

"Ah, no, Ben, they didn't."

"Were they charged?"

"I don't think so."

"I asked if I could press charges."

"I know, but…Look. The Simmons filed paperwork with the courts. They are asking for $75,000."

"I don't have $75,000."

"You need to sell your house."

"But that's mine."

"I know, Ben. But the courts ordered you to pay restitution. We would put it for sale, pay the Simmons, and the rest of the money can go into an account when you get out of here."

Ben shook his head. "This isn't fair."

"Here, sign here so we can get this going."

Joseph put the paperwork in front of Ben. He motioned to the guard who had instructed him earlier about how a prisoner should sign papers. The guard walked over, and Joseph handed Ben a pen. "Sign where my secretary put x's."

Ben signed. He stood and walked away.

Rick was standing right outside as Ben pushed through the door. Ben kept walking in the direction they had walked before. "Ben," Rick said. "Hey, I thought we could go to the library and discuss some programs here."

Ben stopped and turned to him. "They're going to sell my house."

He changed directions again and kept walking.

17

April

April was scheduled for surgery in early February. Because of the anxiety her and her parents felt about her falling behind in her studies, they organized for her to attend school half-day. One day, she would be in morning classes, and the next, in afternoon classes. Her teachers would make sure that they have room for her wheelchair. Her schedule prior to the incident was full, with only enough time for a forty-five-minute lunch. Her mom's flexible schedule as a senior partner attorney specializing in elder law, allowed her to take April to appointments, but they arranged transportation to ease the stress for everyone.

Ashley visited when April told her Marcie had brought over the swag from 10TV. April decided she would use the swag bag on her wheelchair. Ashley asked if she could have the water bottle. They both loved the 10TV news windbreaker, but the baseball cap had a stiff top. They decided April's dad should have it. They talked about when April would return to school. Ashley volunteered to leave their mutual classes early and walk with her. She would help her with projects, share notes, and update April on her team and social events.

On her first day back, April, who usually put her hair in a ponytail or messy bun, took time with her hair and a touch of makeup. She changed her top three times.

67

Omar Armen, the driver, took her wheelchair out of the trunk while April waited in the backseat. When he opened the back passenger door, she scooted to the door, picking up the thigh of her right leg and turning her left leg to dangle out the door. When the driver brought her chair around, Armen helped her transition to her chair. He handed April her 10TV bag containing her books. "Thanks, Mr. Armen."

"No problem, April. Unless something changes, I'll see you at 12:30. You have my number if you need to call for a ride earlier."

April nodded and smiled. She turned her chair to face the school's front door and wheeled to the actuator to open the doors, then stopped in the main hallway and watched students move quickly from one hall to another. To move in a wheelchair in halls where she had briskly walked for the past three years felt weird. Since all of her classes were on the second floor she had to remember where the elevator was located. She never had to use it before.

Everything was divided between before the incident and now. Before, she would gather with her senior friends in the hallway by their lockers; now, she's coming and going at awkward times and not using her locker at all. Before, she and her classmates would work on projects in IB classes. Now, she did some of the projects independently and tried to meld her contributions with what the other students had done or were doing. She met with them on FaceTime if they needed to discuss some things on her half day off. On days she was home for discussions and not at PT, her teachers had her listen in and contribute using Zoom. Before, she would move from class to class en masse. Now, she would leave five minutes early to avoid crowded areas.

April passed by the cafeteria after her last class on her first day back. The first lunch period was in progress, and she noticed Madison and some other Field Hockey teammates were at a table where she could easily reach them. Madison saw her coming and yelled. "April!" She ran over, leaned down to hug her, and walked with her to the table.

Everyone said hi, and they were glad to see her. April asked, "How's softball practice going?"

Last year, April was on the softball team as the second-string shortstop. She mostly sat on the bench and rooted for the others. Today, one of the other girls told her about a freshman who played shortstop on the JV team and hoped the coach would put her on varsity. The talk shifted to a junior on the team, who was required to sit out for six weeks because she was caught vaping in school. April noticed the time. "Guys gotta go. My ride should be here."

"April, you're so lucky to get out now."

April wasn't sure how to respond to that. She grinned, backed her chair out, and turned it toward the front doors.

***

During physical therapy, April had graduated to using medium weights. She felt stronger in her upper body. She added extra weight when Tessa let her. Tessa would ice her arms and shoulders before she went home.

Next, laying on her back, Eric encouraged her to lift her left leg. She concentrated. Her hip felt as if she had a twenty-pound weight tied to her leg. "Is it okay if I put my hands under me?"

"Sure."

Grunting with the effort, she lifted her leg an inch off the table. "Great, April! You did it."

Now, let's put a band around your right leg and try to lift it."

With her toned arm muscles, she lifted her leg with Eric's assistance. There was a noticeable contrast in the tone between her left and right leg muscles. She asked Eric about the differences and how they could work on that.

"April, we are cautiously optimistic your right leg will respond better once the bullet is removed, then we'll tone it up."

They would finish up with Tessa bending and massaging her legs so the muscles and tendons would stay supple.

***

That night, with her dad working late, April and her mom ate alone at dinner. "You look tired."

"I am. I think after dinner, I'll go to bed."

"Have you decided what you will do for your extended essay?"

"Not yet. I need to talk to my psych and English teachers."

"What are you thinking?"

"Something about the media's effect on people."

"Where's this coming from?

April shrugged. "If you do, I'll bet the producer who sent you those things would talk to you."

"Marcie Reynolds?"

"Yes. How do you feel things are going at school?"

"It's different. I see my friends during class, and Ashley walks to some classes with me."

"And Madison?"

"I stopped and talked to her and the girls on the softball team before I left today. They told me about a dynamite freshman at shortstop."

"But?"

"I don't know. I'm there, but I'm not part of the team anymore."

"What about classes? Do you feel you've caught up?"

"I'm good. That's where I'm the most normal. Most of the time, everyone is sitting down. We're starting Hamlet in English. We're going to perform it. I'd like to be Ophelia, but I'll ask to be the queen.

"So, you can be sitting." Her mom laughed. "You're so clever."

"Mom, what if I can't go to prom or graduation?"

"The doctors are being optimistic about your recovery after the surgery. You know what your dad says?"

"We take things as they come."

"Right."

"Mom, I still can't figure it out. Why me?"

"What do you mean?"

"That guy, Franklin, according to Madison, had people going to his house for years. Why would he shoot me?"

Her mom put her fork down, folded her arms, and took a deep breath. "I wish I could give you some peace about that. I'm not sure. I can only guess you were in the wrong place at the wrong time."

April bowed her head and nodded.

18

Ben

Ben, Brody and several other inmates were ushered into a greenhouse. The greenhouse stood on the opposite side of the grounds where Ben was familiar. Brody pointed out to him the gardens spread nearby. Instructions were given to the men to line up on different sides of the worktable. Professor Dr. Knight stood at the head of the table.

"Gentlemen, we are going to start seedlings to use in your gardens. In front of you are seed pods, trays, and dirt. I will bring around seeds in a little while. You are going to fill each seed pod three quarters full. When I bring seeds around, you will place two seeds in each pod unless I tell you specifically another number. Men, we are going to grow enough food to feed everyone here at the prison. Some of you will water the future plants, but we decide that later. Please commence with filling the seed pods."

Ben stood with his hands by his sides, observing as the other men put their hands in the soil in front of them. He studied Brody as he filled one seed pod at a time. Brody noticed him not filling the seed pods. "What's wrong, Ben?"

"I don't like getting my hands dirty."

"Man, you need to do this or they'll make you go back to custodial work."

"What's wrong, gentlemen? The professor lingered nearby, keeping an eye on them.

"I don't like getting dirt under my fingernails," Ben said.

"Well, hm," the professor rubbed his chin. "Wait a minute." He walked away. Brody turned to look at him. Ben stood facing the table, continuing to observe the other prisoners.

The professor returned and stepped between Ben and Brody. "Here, see if these fit."

He handed Ben a pair of flowered gloves. Ben put them on. He nodded. Brody nudged Ben. When Ben didn't respond, he said, "Thank you, Dr. Knight."

Dr. Knight nodded and continued walking.

"You should've said thank you. You want to keep this assignment."

Ben concentrated on putting soil in the seed pods, being careful not to get any dirt on the table.

After both Brody and Ben finished their third tray of seed pods, Dr. Knight returned. "You boys are being meticulous about filling the seed pods. Good for you. I'm giving you two more trays to fill. You will plant tomatoes, peppers, peas, and we're going to grow tomatillos. The fellas like Mexican food here, so it may be fun."

Brody said, "Thank you, sir. Sounds good."

Ben nodded as he continued filling the seed pods. Dr. Knight put the envelopes of seeds by Brody.

The guards had returned most of the men back to the main prison section while Brody and Ben and two others continued planting seeds. Dr. Knight asked them to come to the first table for a minute. "Trace, Miguel, Brody and Ben, I am going to task you with watering these pods once they are all planted. Be careful not to flood them. The water canisters are over by the sinks in the back of the greenhouse. Brody, I am going to ask you to organize and assign tables.

Brody nodded.

"Finish planting and covering the seeds. Water them just enough to make them damp. Questions? I will be in my office. The guard will come and get me."

"How will be we know we're doing right?" Said Trace.

The professor nodded. "Tell you what. I'll come out, in say, twenty minutes and check. Is that good?"

All four men nodded and returned to their stations.

"There are a lot of seeds here," Ben said.

"Yeah, but they all won't grow," Brody said.

***

When the next warm day arrived, the same four men found themselves escorted to a section of the gardens. The professor instructed them to make trellises for the bean plants. Six-foot poles were arranged with a six-foot gap between them. They received directions to place eye screws in the poles with an eight-inch gap, and then proceed to string wire for the trellises. Ben asked for a pencil and a ruler. The guards eyed each other, but Dr. Knight produced both. Ben moved from one post to another, measuring the placement for the eye screws and drawing an x. When he had reached the third post, one guard said, "The rest of you put eyes screws where Ben put marks.

The other three inmates started to work. When they had three poles done, Brody wired two of the poles to form the first trellis.

"You guys are doing well. I can tell I picked the right men for the job," said Dr. Knight. "When you're done there, start making the lines to plant the beans."

As they worked, Ben said to Brody, "There's a lot of weeds out here."

Brody looked around. "Yeah, so?"

"We'll have to get them out."

"I guess."

"Why don't I hoe and then you could take the weeds out easier."

Brody shrugged. "Yeah, sounds good."

"Did you have a garden where you lived?"

"We lived in the projects, so we had a community garden. Did you?"

Ben shook his head. "No, we didn't have enough space in our yard."

"Yeah, my mom liked to grow rows of carrots after the lettuce was done. Other people grew beets, onions, and green beans. My mom tried peppers for one year. Do you know green peppers turn into red peppers?"

"I don't like either."

Brody stopped pulling weeds and looked up at Ben as he hoed. He smiled and shook his head.

19

Ben

Terry's next session with Ben took place a week later. Rick had breakfast with him and then brought him down to Terry's office. At Rick's knock, they heard, "Enter."

Terry was behind his desk, working on his computer. He looked up. "Come on in, Ben. I just need to finish this sentence."

Ben came in and sat in the chair he had occupied at his first session. Terry closed out his work and came around and joined Ben. He didn't say anything. Ben was looking down and tapping his left arm with his right hand. "What's making you anxious, Ben?"

"I think I'm upset."

"You think."

"Yes."

"Did the lawyer upset you? Rick said you had a meeting after I first talked to you."

"Yes."

"Do you want to tell me what you talked about?"

"They're selling my house."

"I see."

"Do you know anyone on the outside who can help you? Watch over things?"

"My mother died years ago."

"Anyone else?"

Ben shook his head no.

"Is there anyone you trust?"

"Mrs. Yarnell."

"Who is that?"

"She's the librarian I worked for."

"Could you call her and ask her to help you?"

Ben nodded.

"Ben, Rick, and I had a discussion about your potential involvement in the Library Service Program here."

Ben was quiet.

"The warden would look at a list you or the Dayton librarians generate, and he would approve or disapprove the list. It's a known fact that incarcerated individuals have limited access to resources. It contributes to prisoners' inability to adapt when they are released. With your help, Ben, we would increase the prison's access and even add computers for prisoners' use."

Ben didn't respond.

"Ben, are you listening?"

"Yes."

"Will you think about it?"

"Yes."

"Besides, seeing your lawyer, how was your week?"

Ben shrugged.

"Okay. I guess we are done today. Let Rick know what you think, and I'll see you in a week."

Ben nodded, stood, and left the room. Terry sat back in his chair and decided he needed to talk with another counselor who was more experienced with neurodiverse prisoners.

Terry was also concerned because Rick had little time before he would be transferred to a Community Confinement Center to start his reentry into society. They had already delayed his transfer once in hopes he could help Ben. They called it an apprenticeship for what Rick wanted to do after his release. He had his degree in sociology from Wright State before his incarceration and wanted to work with prisoners' adaptation when they were released.

***

Rick sat outside Ben's cell, waiting for him to return from maintenance work. At this particular facility, there was an area where men sit and read or talk. The area was meant for quiet activities because the cells in this area had the doors open for most of the day unless an inmate wanted to close his door. Ben came in and went straight to his cell without acknowledging him. Rick sighed and pushed the chair away from the table. He walked to Ben's cell and leaned up against the doorjamb. Ben had sat down at the desk and opened his book.

"Hey."

Ben ignored him. "Are you mad at me or just not talking?"

"If I wasn't talking, why would I talk to you?"

Rick looked down at his feet and waited. Five minutes dragged by. Brody came back and walked by Rick into the cell. He looked at Rick and then at Ben. "Ben, Rick's here."

"I know."

"So why aren't you talking to him? That's not cool."

Ben's head popped up, and he looked at Brody. Rick said, "Come on, Ben. We need to talk."

Ben stood, leaving his book open, and followed Rick into the open area. Rick returned to where he was sitting before Ben joined him. "Giving everyone the silent treatment isn't going to help you."

"I'm mad."

"Okay. About losing your home?"

"Yes."

"I am sorry about that. It's tough. Is that the only home you've had?"

"Yes. My mom owned it and then me. I wanted to paint the inside. Those girls were trespassing."

Rick leaned forward and pointed at Ben. "That's water under the bridge. Now you have to decide where to go from here. Do you have someone helping you on the outside? Terry can advise you."

"I don't want to see that lawyer again."

"I can't blame you for that."

"You don't?"

"No, but I do want you to stop blaming everyone around here who is trying to help you."

"Terry told me I should ask Mrs. Yarnell if she would help

me."

"Then call her. Do you have anyone else? Friends?"

"No.

"I have something for you. It's a recent catalog of books that libraries use to purchase books. If you decide to work with the Dayton system, you should know what's out there.

***

"When I get out, I want to get myself a nice car. It won't have to be new. But it will be sleek."

Brody was lying on his bunk with his arms folded under his head and his legs crossed. As usual, Ben was sitting at the desk with a book in front of him. "Why?"

Brody almost fell off his bunk when Ben responded. He would normally just let Brody jabber on. "Why? Cars attract women. They get you from one place to another. I could deliver food or be an Uber driver to get me started again."

"Oh."

"What kind of car would you want, Ben?"

"I can't drive."

Brody sat up for this answer. "What? Why not?"

"My mother didn't feel I would make the right decisions because of me being autistic."

"So, how'd you get around?"

"I walked."

"To get groceries and stuff?"

"Yes. My mom had a bike but riding it and carrying groceries was hard. I rode it sometimes to work at the library."

"Man, I'll have to teach you once we both get out of here."

"That would be nice."

Ben went back to his reading, and Brody sat with his legs dangling for a bit.

"We should start replanting some tomatoes and shit next week. We'll keep them in the greenhouse. All the cold weather crops have started. Now we just wait for the soil to warm up."

"Brody, they sold my house."

Brody had never owned a place, so he wasn't sure what to say. "That's tough, man. What did they do with your stuff?"

"It was the last I had of my mom and grandmother. The lady

I worked for, Mrs. Yarnell, cleaned it out and put everything in storage. She had some ladies help her."

"That's good, right?"

"Yeah, she worked with a lawyer to give her access to an account so she could help me. You know, pay for the storage."

"Not the lawyer you had who put you in here, huh?"

"No, a friend of hers."

Brody jumped up. "What ya reading?"

Ben picked up the book and handed it to him. Brody leafed through the pages.

"This looks like some kinda catalog."

"It lists all the books that are out there. I will use it in a class I'm going to take. Rick suggested I look at it. We should have some audiobooks here, too. Terry said some guys can't read well. Some have college degrees, but others can't read at all."

"I've never been much on reading. Hey, let's go to the rec area and get some cards. We can play gin or something if other guys are down there."

"I don't know how."

"Wow. Well, come on. I'll teach you."

"Um, no. I think I'll stay here."

"Okay."

Brody reported to Rick the next day that Ben had talked to him. "Well, it's a start. I saw him sit with you and the other guys at meals."

"He doesn't say much. I tried to get him to play cards, but he wouldn't."

"I don't suspect he will, Brody. Terry says that being social is hard for him. Maybe someday."

***

Terry was finishing up paperwork when Ben arrived for his weekly appointment.

"Be right with you, Ben."

Ben came into the office and sat. He first sat with his hands on the armrests, his back straight, and his feet on the floor. As Terry worked, he crossed his leg, ankle over knee. Terry was watching him, glancing at him from time to time. Ben uncrossed his legs, then crossed his arms. When Terry filed his papers away in a drawer and came around to talk to him, he resumed his first position.

"Are you comfortable, Ben?"

Ben shifted. "Yeah, I'm good."

"Do you want to tell me something?"

"Yes, I did as you said about calling Mrs. Yarnell, and she wrote to me. She took care of everything for me. Her lawyer helped me set up a bank savings account for the remaining funds."

He said this in a monotone, as if he was reciting information.

"That's good, Ben."

Ben nodded.

"Have you thought any more about what you can do here?"

"I want to work with the Dayton Library System."

"Ben, that's great. I'll talk to the warden. He said he thought we could start with a computer in the library, and we could see if we could find a grant for others."

"Would others be able to use the library computer?"

"No, that would be for you to work with the library."

Ben started rocking. "Good."

Terry had never seen Ben do this movement before. "Are you okay? What are you feeling?"

"I don't want others working on that computer. They could mess things up."

"Okay, Ben. The other computers could be in the classrooms when we get them.

"I could take care of them."

"Good idea. Could you teach people to use them? Do you think, Ben?"

"Nope."

"Know your limitations, huh?"

"Yes."

"In the meantime, you'll work in the greenhouse and gardens."

"I like doing that. Brody and I have a system."

"You do? What is it?"

"I hoe, and he gets the weeds after I loosen the ground."

"Good system."

"We're planting tomatoes, peppers, peas, and ...some other

things."

"Sounds good."

"Others are putting in onions, carrots and squash. Professor Knight said we should be able to feed just about everyone in the prison."

"He's a good guy. Do you know he taught at the university for thirty-some years?"

"He's working here now."

"He volunteers his time, Ben."

"Hm. That's good."

"Brody said he's teaching you to play cards."

"He is, but I don't want to play with the other guys yet."

"Okay, why don't you go and just watch until you're comfortable enough to play cards?"

Ben nodded his head.

Later, after cleaning up and going to dinner, Brody told Ben he was going to play cards. Ben got up and followed him. "Are you coming to the rec area, Ben?"

"Terry suggested I watch even if I don't want to play."

"Okay, great."

The rec area was a vast open room with a monitor and comfortable chairs in a U-shape. Three pool tables were on the other side of the room. In the middle were tables and chairs. Sofas and bookshelves containing games, puzzles, a paperback exchange, and magazines lined the two walls. One table was open for Brody and his three friends to play cards. Ben said he'd stand because no other chairs were available. Four guards were stationed to monitor all the activities.

The guys don't play for money. That was against the rules. They play for points and bragging rights. Gin was the game tonight. Ben was standing back, watching. Chee, a slight Asian man with several tattoos in Chinese on his arms, asked Ben what they planted today.

"We got a lot of the tomatoes in. We'll more to put in tomorrow."

"How many varieties are being planted?"

Brody said, "Four, I think. Right, Ben?"

"Yeah, Professor Knight said the early ones should be ready

in July."

"Wow, that's great. They won't let me go and plant."

Ben said, "Why not?"

"You see these thumbs? They're black."

Looking at Chee's thumbs, Ben said, "No, they're not."

The men laughed. "No, Ben. Not really. He means he can't grow things." Brody said.

Ben had eased closer to them.

Chee said, "Ben, do you know what it means when someone has sticky fingers?"

"It means they've been making something."

"Maybe, but it also means they are stealing or cheating at cards."

Chee's forehead was raised, and his smiling eyes were fixed on one of the other players across the table.

"Well, isn't it Pinto and his motley crew?"

The guys looked up, and a few with their backs to the voice turned to see Keno. They kept playing their game, taking turns glancing at each other.

Keno walked around the table. He'd occasionally lean on one of the men's chairs, pretending to watch the game. Leaning in, he whispered in Chee's ear. Being a large, barrel-chested, broad-shouldered man, he pushed Chee forward. Chee brushed his ear as if to swat at a mosquito. Keno laughed.

Ben instinctively stepped back from Keno's orbital movement. He watched as Keno stopped behind Brody. Keno reached over Brody's shoulder, pulled a card from his hand, and threw it on the table. "Pinto, don't take so long. That's the right card."

"Don't call him that."

Keno stopped laughing, straightened, and glared at Ben. "What did you say?"

"Don't call him that."

Keno straightened and advanced toward Ben. Ben took a few steps back. Three guards dashed to the card players' table. One placed himself between Keno and Ben. The other two flanked Keno. "Now, why would you want to cause trouble, Keno? You just got out of solitary. You're about to be banned from this rec area. Let the guys play cards."

Red-faced Keno, breathing hard, looked at the guard facing

him. Ben saw that his fists were clenched. The guard on his right said, "Let's escort Keno to his cell, Mac. He's done in here tonight." The guard on Keno's left said, "Good idea. Come on, Keno."

As Keno left, his eyes were fixed on Ben.

Ben was backed up to the wall. He had his arms crossed against his chest and was holding his breath. The remaining guard walked to him. "Ben. It's okay. He's gone."

Ben closed his eyes and then reopened them. He took a breath. He was frozen in place. Brody said, "Guys, I'm going to get Ben back to our cell."

Chee and the others nodded. Brody put his hand on Ben's arm. Ben took a verbal inhale and backed away from Brody. "Come on, Ben. We never talked about Keno. 'Bout time we did."

Ben hugged himself and started tapping his arm. "It's okay, Ben. Keno is gone."

The men at the card table looked at each other. Chee said, "Brody, you want us to deal you out?"

"Nah. Ben will be okay when I get him back to our cell."

Ben nodded.

Leading the way to the exit door., Brody said, "Come on, Ben."

20

Marcie and Greg

Marcie and Greg took the hour-long trip south to Springridge. When Marcie drove down to deliver the swag bag of goodies , April struck her as being so young. They talked over tea and cookies that Adele had helped April to prepare for when Marcie arrived. April told Marcie she planned to go to Miami to play Field Hockey with her friends. She didn't know what she wanted to study, but now wondered if physical therapy might be a good major. Marcie asked what her parents did. April mentioned her mom held the position of a senior attorney, specializing in trusts and estates. Her dad did research on curing Alzheimer's and Aphasia. Marcie voiced surprise April didn't want to follow in either of her parents' footsteps. April shrugged.

The situation still bothered Marcie. The life of the young athlete was altered, and the individual responsible was currently in prison. However, judging from the video of Franklin's arraignment, the questions about why the girls were on his property remained unanswered. Was Franklin just another person who shouldn't have had a gun? Marcie still sensed there was more here.

After Marcie and Greg discussed her visit with April, Greg said, "Well, let's go down and take a look see."

"What are we looking for?"

"I don't know. The lay of the land. The town culture. You can sometimes get a feel for a place by finding its watering hole or local restaurant. Let's go down and have lunch and hang out for a bit."

It turned out that there was a crowded breakfast/ lunch place in the center of town. A facade was added to the building, making it look like it was part of the original town. The Lancaster white tabletops and black hairpin cafe chairs added a sophisticated touch to the well-lit interior. Soft-colored modern art graced the white walls.

A female server in her late twenties came to their table. She brought them water, asked if they wanted straws, and gave them menus. When she returned for their orders, she said, "Excuse me, aren't you on television?"

Greg turned from his menu and said, "Yes, channel ten news."

"I thought so. What brings you down here?"

"My producer Marcie and I are here looking into the Halloween incident and we like the town."

The server looked perplexed. "What incident?"

"The girl who was shot by the guy who lived alone?" Marcie said.

Oh, that. That guy and his mother were strange. And their house? Everyone here thought he got off easy."

"How did he get off easy?" Asked Greg.

The server looked around. "I'd better take your orders. My boss will notice me just talking and not handing in an order."

"Okay. Look at my menu like you're answering a question. How did he get off easy?"

She looked at his menu. "Everyone around here believes that he should have faced charges for attempted murder. Now what can I get you?"

After Marcie and Greg placed their order, Greg said, "What was wrong with the house?"

Marcie shrugged. "Remember? You said when you saw the video, it was a mess."

"After breakfast, let's walk around a bit."

The little town consisted of one street of small shops and restaurants, a bank in the middle, a park with sculpture and picnic tables on one end, and a large stone government building with marble pillars on the other. Marcie stopped in one shop she thought looked interesting. It offered some unique kitchen and dining items that she purchased. Greg waited outside. They walked around the town square. When they returned to their car, they continued their tour, starting with the house where Ben lived.

They parked by the Sweet Memories Garden Cemetery. "Shall we stroll through the cemetery?"

"After that breakfast, I could use more walking. That meal might last me until tomorrow," Marcie said.

"It won't take us very long," Greg said. "There's the fence. At least that way, it's only a block long."

"There are some ancient monuments here, Greg. This one is from the eighteen hundreds and looks like a family plot."

"There are markers signifying WWII, but I don't see any markers more recent than that."

"It could be full if the family plots were the rest of the grave sites."

After the brief walk through the cemetery, Marcie and Greg crossed the street to Ben's former home. The privets were removed, and the fence taken down. The house, except for the porch, looked fine. A good power washing had removed its mossy appearance.

Greg took a few pictures of the house and its yard. "Looks like someone is looking to sell it."

"Or it has been sold and getting ready to be flipped."

They continued to stroll down to Brueberry Lane. The houses ranged from a 1930s Art Deco to Cape Cods. Many structures were made of brick, some had white siding, and others had gray cedar shingles. The lawns were manicured, with one or two exceptions. Poplar trees lined the streets. A lawn mower was heard in the distance. Besides a few kids going by on bikes, they didn't see many people.

"This seems to be more of a bedroom community to Columbus." said Marcie.

"At one time, it was surrounded by farms and small industries. It seems people from Midtown and other professionals have made it graduate from a population of farmers and small-town ownership to what it is today." Greg said.

When Marcie gave him a questioning look, he said, "I did some checking. It once boasted small kitchen appliance manufacturing, farming, and industrial manufacturing. The small kitchen appliance manufacturer is gone. Farming continues, but it's more or less a big owner/business effort. Industrial manufacturing still exists and does all it can to support the schools. People who have gravitated here are professionals who work in Columbus, Cincinnati or Dayton."

"They have a mixture of professional and university populations mixed with the long-term residents."

"Yes."

Greg and Marcie walked in silence for a block. "But how did a young woman end up getting shot on Halloween by a man who seemed harmless?"

Greg shrugged. "Dunno. How about Sean and I talk to some more folks here?"
Marcie nodded.

21

Barb Yarnell

The Springridge Library was a refurbished 1920s Art Deco style, yellow brick building. Once Springridge built the new high school, the building became a unique town library. Barb Yarnell worked hard to welcome people and turned the old place into a comfortable and inviting community center.

Greg and Seth climbed the stairs to the front and opened the double doors to find Mrs. Yarnell's office immediately to their left. Greg smiled at the lady at the information desk as she welcomed them to the Springridge Library.

"Mrs. Yarnell said she would be right down. I just need to call her and let her know you're here. You can wait in her office if you like."

Greg reached down to turn the doorknob to the office. The homey outer office, carpeted in a honey brown, had a central feature of a red brick fireplace. Comfortable chairs in a rustic red sat on either side. A dark oak office door bearing the stencil of Principal was open, and inside was a solid wood desk and bookshelves. Cream-colored walls complimented the dark wood of the overflowing bookshelves.

"Where do you want to set up, Seth?"

"I like the fireplace area. I'll go back to the truck and get some lights."

He set up his camera before the fireplace and left to get the rest of his supplies. Greg stood looking at the art decorating the walls. He read the names of the artists. He wondered if former students here at the old high school created the paintings.

"Yes. We kept those and added more in the hallways."

Greg turned to see a woman who was about five foot two with short, peppered hair and bright, red-rimmed glasses. She walked toward him with her hand outstretched. "Hi, I'm Barb Yarnell."

"Greg Stanton."

"Yes. It's nice to have you."

"According to my photographer, it would be nice to record the interview before the fireplace."

"That's fine. Would you both like some coffee? I could ask Anna, the lady at the Information Desk, go to the coffee room and make you some. Second thought, why don't I show you around?"

Seth came in with lights and shades. "We're going to take a tour of the library."

"Okay."

Seth walked over to his camera and hoisted it to his shoulder. Some of the former classrooms were meeting rooms. The blackboards were now turned into whiteboards. "We had to take all the blackboards and put them up higher. People are taller now."

"I saw that when I reached for your office doorknob," Greg said.

Mrs. Yarnell laughed. "Well, yes. For some of us, that doorknob is still in the right place."

Original wood seats filled the auditorium. The curtains of the small stage looked new. "We had a community theater that used this space, but somehow people lost interest."

It could be that as the population shifted, people didn't have time.

"Could be. Occasionally, people rent it for dance recitals. I love watching the little kids perform."

"Shall we go back to your office?"

Mrs. Yarnell, pulled from her pensiveness, nodded.

As Seth set up his lights and tested the microphones, Greg and Mrs. Yarnell chatted about books and the changes in the community.

Finally, as they were ready to start, Greg received a text from Marcie to make sure he asked if Ben had ever called the police.

"Ready to start the interview?" Greg asked Seth.

Seth nodded.

Greg: Mrs. Yarnell, how long have you been Library Director?

Mrs. Yarnell: Almost thirty years.

Greg: Have you seen a lot of change in Springridge?

Mrs. Yarnell: Yes and no. There is a protective pride that has existed in Springridge. The community would like to believe that its small-town quality still exists, and in some ways, it has.

Greg: (Nodding to encourage her.) How so?

Mrs. Yarnell: Springridge was a small town surrounded by farms for most of its history. The suburbs of Columbus now have reached us, and it has turned into a bedroom community of professionals who want their children to have an excellent education and a safe place to grow up.

Greg: Is that a bad thing?

Mrs. Yarnell: No, of course not. There is a deserved snobbery about it. But there's also another side of that snobbery. When the majority number of residents were people who worked and lived here, people didn't have to lock their doors. They protected each other. They supported each other in bad times and accepted each other's curious ways. Everyone watched over each other's kids. It was almost ideal. I used to love watching kids walk home from school. When I left work, I would see kids playing outside until dark. Now, I hardly see the kids outside. The standards for education are higher because professionals have moved in and work in a city or at one of the universities. Young people are under so much pressure to go to college. We have tutors here after school, and they are always busy. The board of education boasts ninety-nine percent of the students go to college. Only a few of the kids come back here to live. The people who originally lived here may still be in their homes but have a more challenging time staying because of the property taxes. Their kids who grew up here may not be able to afford a home because the house prices have increased. I can't complain the library is well supported, but I see the changes.

Greg: Ben Franklin worked here before he went to prison.

Mrs. Yarnell: Yes, he did.

Greg: What was he like?

Mrs. Yarnell: He was a good employee. Susie Waxman came to me when Ben was a junior in high school. She said he was a loner. The kids bullied him because he was different. And then there was his mother. She used to come into the library with that silly bird on her shoulder, but I ignored it. Occasionally, it would be loud, but she hushed it. Her name was Dinah. She cared for Ben, but poor dear, she had her problems. The three of us worked together to give Ben a safe place. He worked here his senior year, putting books away and doing small chores. He made enough to attend and graduate from Columbus State and gained more skills to work here as an IT. We threw a little graduation party here in the meeting room.

Greg: How'd he react to that?

Mrs. Yarnell: I remember he didn't say much. He smiled a lot but said nothing much but thank you. Over and over, he said thank you.

Greg: Did he show any aggressiveness or violent behavior?

Mrs. Yarnell: No, never.

Greg: Can you tell me what happened when his mother died?

Mrs. Yarnell: Oh my, that was an awful time for him. Ben must have worried when he was a kid that someone would come and take him away. Susie once told me Child Services made visits. The neighbors reported to the police an awful stench coming from the house. You know, Dinah's neighbors were always helping if they could. Those neighbors moved out, and new ones came in. Ben did his best to cut the grass or do repairs on the house. I remember him taking out books on house repair. Mr. Switzer, who owned Springridge Hardware, went over to help him and took extra tools. Mr. Switzer sold out. Now, there are several small shops, and people go to the big hardware stores.

Anyway, when the report came in about the odor, the police went over to Ben's house to check out the complaints, but he wouldn't let them in.

Greg: The smell must have been awful.

Mrs. Yarnell: The police, when they called me, said it backed them up when he opened the door.

Greg: Geez.

Mrs. Yarnell: After the police called me, I went over to see Ben. He had stopped coming to work because he was afraid the police would break in. I met him on the front porch of his house. It was awful. You could smell death through the windows. I asked him what happened. He said his mother had made dinner, stood to clean up, and collapsed. He tried to help her, but she didn't respond. I didn't ask what he did. It didn't matter at this point. I explained that he wasn't respecting his mother's memory by keeping her in the house. He needed to put her to rest properly. He cried. I told him I would help. And I did. I contacted Donnelly's Funeral home in town. They came that afternoon and took Dinah Franklin away. Susie and I sent flowers so he could mourn adequately. The library staff members, Susie Waxman, and I were the only ones at her funeral. Ben didn't think we should have any services for her, but we asked Reverend Seabright from the Methodist Church to say a few words for him. He did. Susie and I made dinner at my house for him as we aired out his house. Ben came to work the next day.

Greg: How do you explain what he did on Halloween?

Mrs. Yarnell: Ben and his mom were harassed for years. It first started when Ben was in high school. The high school kids egged their house. They soaped their windows. After Ben graduated high school, the high school seniors started knocking on the doors and running. It first started in the spring. Then it gradually spread throughout the year. Anytime the kids felt ornery. It became a thing. A rite of passage. They called it a senior tradition.

Greg: Did parents realize what was going on? Did Ben do anything about it? Did he call the police?

Mrs. Yarnell: I don't think Ben did. His mother did. She would go down to the police station and raise a stink. The police would tell her they would send a patrol car. Ben must have decided there wasn't anything the police would do. He let the lawn go, and the bushes grow high to scare the kids away.

Greg: And parents?

Mrs. Yarnell shrugged her shoulders. "Ben is nearing forty. It could be some of those parents were in school with him. Anyway, Ben was a good worker. I had no problems with him. He kept to himself and did his work."

22

Susie Waxman

Greg and Seth walked up the gray cedar-shingled, well-cared-for Cape Cod driveway. "Doesn't this house look like it should belong to a librarian?" Greg said to Seth. Seth smiled and nodded. Greg knocked on the bright yellow door.

Seth smiled and nodded.

The door swung open, and a tall, sturdy-looking woman invited them in. "I know who you are. I enjoy following your stories whenever you are on 10TV. Welcome, Greg."

"Thank you, Mrs. Waxman. This is Seth Lanberry, my photographer."

Greg and Seth stepped into her home. "Greg and Seth, this is my husband, Ted. He wanted to meet you, too. He told the whole neighborhood you were coming."

Greg grasped Ted's extended hand. "It's good to meet you too, Ted."

Seth also shook hands with Ted. "So what brings you here, Greg? Susie said you wanted to hear about Sonny Franklin."

"Are you aware he was convicted of felonious assault?"

Ted nodded. "We're doing a follow-up story about him."

"Greg and Seth, I made some coffee and cookies. Why don't we go into the three-season room, and you can tell me what you need."

Greg and Seth followed Mrs. Waxman through her mouth-watering scented kitchen into a cozy room surrounded by windows. Ratan white furniture with bright flowered cushions decorated the space. A plate of chocolate chip cookies and a pot of coffee sat on the table. Three mugs waited to be filled.

"Mrs. Waxman, you didn't have to go to so much trouble."

"I feel like you're an old friend. Sit."

Before she sat down, Susie Waxman poured coffee and handed Greg and Seth a napkin and a cookie. "Mrs. Waxman, Barb Yarnell at the Springridge Library told me you could tell me about Ben Franklin's high school days. She seemed to believe he had a rough time of it."

"Barb has been a good friend to Ben. She and I have worked to help him since he was fifteen. We were surprised his attorney didn't call us to help him during the trial."

"Why?"

"We could watch too much Law and Order. We thought we could tell the court what brought him to do what he did. The lawyer never called us back."

Seth had set up the camera as they were talking. "Seth here will go about his business as we talk, Mrs. Waxman. He's used to being ignored. He's going to put a microphone on you. Is where she's sitting okay, Seth?"

"It's fine. I need to add another light or two, but we're good because the sun isn't too bright in this room today."

Seth placed a microphone on Mrs. Waxman's bright pink blouse. "I like the colors, Mrs. Waxman. They go nicely with the cushions."

"Thank you, Seth."

After Seth finished testing the sound and lighting, Greg started the interview. Tell me about Ben, Mrs. Waxman.

Mrs. Waxman: Ben was small for his age when he entered high school. We called him Sonny back then. As far back as elementary school, the kids had already marked him as someone they could bully. The middle school librarian, Marty Westwood, warned me about the kids who struggled. We had an agreement to do so. High school brought the same treatment for Ben, but worse. At the middle school, the kids seemed to ignore him and only tease him every so often. But he couldn't get through the cafeteria at the high school without someone tripping him or taking his lunch.

Greg: Because of his size?

Mrs. Waxman: That was only part of it. His mother might have caused some of it.

Greg: His mother?

Mrs. Waxman: Dinah Franklin was known to all the kids. She insisted on walking Ben to school at fifteen. You know how kids are, but Dinah made it worse. She walked him to school with a parrot on her shoulder. That parrot would squawk at the kids as she and Ben walked. If the parrot wasn't squawking, Dinah—Greg, Dinah Franklin had bipolar disorder. Sometimes, she would be talking a mile a minute about everything. Ben would listen. Other times, she became nasty and said mean things to the kids. Ben would try to stop her, but she would yell at or mock him.

Greg: How did Ben handle that?

Mrs. Waxman: Ben believed he needed to take care of his mom. He told me that his dad left when he was three. He was a history professor at the Denison University but found an opportunity at another college and left to teach there.

Greg: Why didn't he take them with him?

Mrs. Waxman: (putting her hands together) Another teacher once told me, and I am not sure how true this is, but he realized Dinah had bipolar disorder, and he learned that the disorder could be genetic. He didn't want to deal with both his wife and son having the disorder, so he left. He bought the house for them and sent them money through spousal and child support and had no further contact.

Greg: That had to be hard on the kid.

Mrs. Waxman: (nodding) I think so too. Anyway, Ben felt it was his job to care for his mom. He couldn't fight the kids who made fun of his mom or him. He tolerated them.

Greg: So, how did he cope with school?

Mrs. Waxman: We, the faculty, protect kids like him as much as possible. We talked to the kids when we caught them. We taught kindness and tolerance. But as the librarian, I always tried to give kids like Ben a safe place to be.

Greg: What do you mean?

Mrs. Waxman: I kept food in my office when they didn't want or refuse to go to the cafeteria. Ben faced greater challenges than most. One time, Ben was put upside down in a trash can in the cafeteria. According to the faculty member who saw the incident, my goodness, what was his name?" Mrs. Waxman sat for a moment, looking up. "Oh yes. Mr. Wisemen.

According to him, Ben never yelled or anything. Somehow, he righted himself by knocking the can over, and crawling out. Ben then just walked over to the group of laughing kids and threw himself at the bully who did it to him. Bennet was his name. Darnell Bennet, he's a police officer now. Both were suspended for fighting. When he returned, Sonny still had some bruises on his face and arms.

Greg: That doesn't seem right.

Mrs. Waxman: Another time, Darnell put Ben on top of one bank of lockers to get even. I came upon him when I heard him say my name. I looked up, and there he was. He couldn't get down. It was already six o'clock. I had stayed late to catch up with some grants I was writing. That's when I brought him into the library crew.

Greg: Did that happen to a lot of kids?

Mrs. Waxman: The administration helped me provide a comfortable place for them to sit and do their homework. I gave some kids jobs. Ben served as one of my aides. When libraries had more books, he would shelve them for me or check books in and out. When more computers were bought for the library, kids like Ben would help me with them. They knew more about them than I did.

Greg: So, Ben wasn't really social.

Mrs. Waxman: (smiling) No, I encouraged him when he was a senior to ask one of the other library aides to go to the prom. We offered to pay for a ride and a place to eat. We wanted to make it memorable for them. But he said no. I never knew why.

Greg: That's rough.

Mrs. Waxman: The teachers reported Ben's situation to child services once. Some were convinced when he was a sophomore that his home life wasn't what it should be.

Greg: What happened?

Mrs. Waxman: You know his mother, Dinah, suffered from bipolar disorder. It's a tricky disorder. Dinah had days where she was high energy. She insisted that Ben should have rigorous studies. She would write to the teachers and have ideas about how to increase his challenges because she decided he needed them. Other times, Ben took care of himself. He would bring peanut butter sandwiches for lunch." (chuckling) "One time, he came to school with a light pink shirt, and I noticed his socks were a light pink tint. I commented on his shirt. He said his mom was sick, and he did the wash and put a colored towel in with the white towels and his shirt. I guess the colored towel was red. Those times were when his mom was low.

Greg: What did children's services do?

Mrs. Waxman: Nothing. It is possible that she was having a good day when they visited or talked to Dinah. We wished we had a chance to tell the judge about Ben's background and all. You know, be character witnesses.

23

Marcie and Greg

Marcie and Greg met to begin work on the documentary and discuss the consumer complaints that were phoned in and categorized them into news stories, or phone calls that could alleviate the problem for the viewer, or areas requiring additional research.

"We've accumulated a lot of information for the documentary, but I'm not sure where to start. We need to be certain what we want to accomplish," Marcie said. "We can only create one teaser and forty-eight to forty-three minutes of content.

Greg sat back in his chair and laughed. "Now that's a change."

"Stop teasing."

"Okay, why don't we start with the news piece of the event?"

"If we start with information about bullying, or a dramatic opening, ..."

"It will play like 'Inside Edition'," Greg said.

"Yes."

"Or Law and Order. Don don Ta DON!"

Marcie laughed. "We definitely don't want that. We do need to recap what happened on Halloween Night."

"Should we start out in Springridge?"

"At what site? The park? City Hall? The courthouse?"

"No, to the courthouse. It wasn't decided there."

"Good point."

"We don't want to give the impression the town is a horrible place," said Greg.

"Because it's not."
"Right."
"But it was the town that let a bullying situation…"
"Become a tradition."

Once they decided on the opening and introduction, they had to determine how much time to give each interview. Then they discussed each interview and its value since it would help to determine what quotes they would include. They had to discuss if and how they would include an interview with Ben since interviews and cameras are prohibited in the prison. Greg thought pictures of the house pre-renovation and the prison could be shown with Greg as a voiceover of what Ben tells him. Marcie was curious if it would be journalistically correct.

"But we need to use some of what he says to keep the documentary unbiased."

"Could we petition the prison to be able to at least tape his voice? And we need to Interview April's father."

Greg wrote a note and nodded.

"We'll storyboard it and see how it falls. Agreed?" Greg looked at his watch. "Greek or Italian? I'm starved."

"Want to try Lemon Grass Chicken?"

"What, Tai? You?"

"I tried it last week. It was good."

"Like I said, Greek or Italian?"

"Greek. Salad and a chicken bowl."

"Great."

He left to order their dinner. Marcie asked herself what the purpose of the documentary was. She wanted to be clear in her mind so when they chose comments and facts for the script and storyboard, the resulting message was evident. Over dinner, she would discuss with Greg the possibility of achieving their purpose in video and in the script.

Greg came back into the editing bay. "It should be here in twenty minutes."

"Let's go into the conference room."

"Okay."

"Greg, what is the purpose of our documentary?"

"I thought we agreed how a bullying situation became a tradition."

"But how do we accomplish this without making it appear as though this is a singular event?

"Remember how we showed hazing at one of the universities that turned deadly? We concentrated on the one university, but in the end, we brought in other incidents throughout the entire state."

"The young man's parents were proud of the piece, even though the university and fraternity questioned hated it."

"Yes, but we interviewed the boys involved because they weren't charged yet. Here, the guy's in jail."

"We didn't enact it."

"But we took video of the fraternity house and the university."

"True."

"Okay, why don't we start at the house as it was?"

"And have Susie Waxman narrate what it was like for Ben during his teen years."

"Will this be at the beginning or the intro?"

"The beginning. I still don't know how to start it."

"Why not let me start with statistics about bullying?"

"Is there an expert like a psychologist or professor who can provide us with the needed information?"

"Okay, but it will lengthen the piece." Greg stood.

"Are you going to do research it now?"

"No, Marcie. I'm going to check and see if our food has arrived."

24

Ben

"Ben, you have a visitor."

Ben looked up from the book he was reading and asked, "Who is it?"

The prison guard who was relaying the message shrugged. "He was scheduled. Didn't you check?"

"I wasn't expecting anyone, so no."

"Well, come on, or I'll tell the guy you won't see him."

The chair scraped as Ben placed his bookmark and stood. He remembered Brody was still working on the garden project.

As Ben walked into the interview area, he didn't see anyone he would expect to visit. A broad-shouldered, tall man stood. As Ben walked closer, the man's face was familiar. He was wearing a plaid sports coat and navy-blue slacks. He was tan and had the posture of a once-upon-a-time athlete. Ben stood behind the chair, keeping it and the table separating them.

"Hi, my name is Greg Stanton. I'm with WCMS News."

Greg extended his hand.

"You're a reporter."

Still, with his hand out, Greg said, "Yes."

"What do you want?"

Greg withdrew his hand. "Can we sit?"

"Not until I know what you want."

"Okay. We're investigating more about what happened on the night you shot April Simmons. My producer, Marcie Reynolds, and I want to look into it because we feel the entire story didn't come out."

"It didn't."

"Okay, well, let's sit and talk about it."

Ben nodded, pulled the chair out, and sat. Looking up at Greg, he said, "They sold my house."

"Mr. Franklin."

"Ben."

"Ben, we want to do an interview with you so you have a chance to tell your side of the story. We intend to do a documentary about how bullying can be systemic, and possibly your story is an example of that. What do you think? (Showing Ben his phone.) We have permission from the Director of the Ohio Department of Rehabilitation and Correction to make an audio tape if you agree.

Ben nods.

Greg pushes record. "Ben.Do agree to being taped for this interview?"

Ben: Yes.

Greg: Ben, I've been talking to Barb Yarnell and Susie Waxman. They both said you had a rough time. They both said you been… harassed since high school. Did your attorney bring any of it up in court?

Ben: No.

Greg: Do you have any reason why?

Ben, not making eye contact with Greg, shook his head no.

Greg: Ben, you have to say no, if that is your answer.

Ben: No.

Greg: What are your thoughts about how everything turned out?

Ben: I don't have any feelings about anything.

Greg: What do you do in here?

Ben: I work in the garden. I like to hoe. Brody will pull weeds after I loosen them up, and I'll take care of the library soon as IT.

Greg: You did that for Barb Yarnell and the Springridge Library.

Ben: Yes.

Greg: Anything else?

Ben: I may take some classes, and I can play cards.

Greg looked confused, and then he grinned.

Greg: What type of cards do you play?

Ben: Gin.

Greg: Are you good at it?

 Ben: Brody says I'm learning.

Greg: And who is Brody?

Ben: We live in our cell together.

Greg: Ben, what goals do you have?

 Ben looked up. "Goals?"

Greg: I mean. When you get out?

Ben: They sold my house for restitution. Mrs. Yarnell helped me with the banking and the rest.

Greg: Will you go back to the Springridge library?

Ben: (looking to the side) "I don't know."

Greg: Ben, you could get out in three years. Could you rebuild your life somewhere else?

Ben: Where would I go? (Ben looked at his hands.) I can't drive, but Brody said he'd teach me. He said I have to have a dream car. They attract girls.

Greg: I've heard that. Are you sorry you hurt April Simmons?

(Ben folded his arms across his chest.)

Ben: Those girls were trespassing. I wanted them to leave me alone. I didn't want my house egged or for them to knock on my doors or windows. I didn't want them to put wax on my windows. Someone put cow manure in my yard. I wanted it to stop.

 Greg: Why didn't you call the police?

Ben: My mom used to call them. But nothing happened. People kept it up.

Greg: Mrs. Waxman told me one guy who bothered you in high school is now a police officer. Did that factor into your choice to not contact the police?

Ben: (shrugging) "I don't know. Maybe."

Greg: Did the attorney you had to bring anything up in court about kids constantly bothering your house?

Ben: He said it irrelevant.

Greg: Ben, is there anything you want people to know about you?

Ben: (sitting for a moment, looking off to the side). I had a right to be left alone in my house. I wanted to paint the inside.

Greg: Yes, you did have the right to be left alone.

Ben: It's almost dinner time. I like the food here except lima beans and red meat. It's not good for you.

Greg: You said you were going to take classes? What kind?

Ben: Library and Information Science.

Greg: What will you do with that?

Ben: They want me to work with the library here.

Greg: That's great, Ben.

Ben: I worked at the library in Springridge for seventeen years.

Greg: (pausing and sitting back in the chair) Can you tell me what happened that Halloween?

Ben: I didn't turn my light on like you're supposed to if you want kids to come to your house. Some kids came into my yard about six and spread manure over my porch and front steps. It took me about an hour to clean it up. I put it in a trash bag and put in a container, but it still smelled. I washed down the porch and steps with a hose. About eight, kids came and yelled, "Trick or Treat!" I didn't answer my door. They went to the side windows and soaped them. (Ben shrugged.) At least they didn't put dirty words on them. It was quiet for a while and then I heard a thud on my front door. I waited for a while and then went around the back to the front. Someone threw a rotten pumpkin against the front door and on my porch. I cleaned that up and took out the hose again to wash it down. That's when I took out my father's gun from the locked closet, loaded it, and went upstairs to my bedroom window.

Greg: What time was this about?

Ben: It was past nine.

Greg: What were the times of trick or treat?

Ben: Six to Eight.

Greg: So it was dark now.

Ben: Yes.

Greg: Then what happened?

Ben: I was about to put the gun away when I heard some girls talking in my yard. I watched them as they went to my porch. They knocked on my front door, soaped it, and ran off the porch. They stopped right at the gate. One of the girls said she needed to go back. They were standing at the gate whispering. I shot at the bushes to scare them away. They screamed. I shot my gun again at the bushes. I waited another hour, locked up the gun, and went to bed. I needed to work the next day.

Greg: When did you find out you shot the girl?

Ben: When the police came the next day.

Greg looked over Ben's shoulder. The guard nodded to him. "Looks like time is up for me. Ben, thank you for talking with me."

Ben nodded. He pushed back his chair and stood. He walked away, stopped, and turned around. With his head down as if to bow, he said, "It was nice to meet you." He then turned toward the exit door.

25

Complaints

Not all individuals were pleased that Greg and Seth were conducting interviews in Springridge. Mayor Rodgers contacted Station Manager Jacob Brossner to express his dissatisfaction with his news team bringing up a rare incident that could besmirch the reputation of his town. Since Brossner was out of town, Kim Wolford handled the call, and another call came from the City Council President. He alleged that there were reports of Greg and Seth harassing people on the streets of his fine city.

"Besmirch?" Greg said, "Who uses that word?"

"Greg, the mayor of Springridge, does," Kim said. "Exactly what were you doing?"

Seth, Greg, Marcie, and Kim discussed the complaints in the conference room.

"I had my camera to set up to photograph some local shots like the park, and a few people approached and inquired what we were doing there. I told him we were doing a news story," Seth said, "Like I always do."

"Yeah, one guy asked why. I told him it related to how Ben Franklin was treated as a kid and how people kept bothering him as he became an adult. Then I asked him if he or maybe his kids took part in that senior tradition," Greg said.

Kim shook her head.

"The guy told Greg Franklin should have been tried for attempted murder and we needed to leave or he'd call the police."

"But you were in the park?" Kim said.

"Yes, I wanted to get a shot of the sculpture there. It was

nice. I guess a local artist did it."

"We relocated and were taking a shot of Franklin's former house, and a neighbor came out. Again, he asked what we were doing, and we told him the same thing. The guy said it wasn't cool that we were dredging up what happened, and he, for one, was glad Franklin was gone."

Marcie said, "Greg, it might be understandable for a neighbor. The house was considered an eyesore."

"True. Hey, we met a local police detective. He stopped by. The mayor might not think he could be a candidate for the local welcome committee. Not a very cordial officer."

"What were you doing, then?"

"We were taking video of the outside of the library. A lady came out and came up to us and asked us what we were doing. She had seen us in the library talking to Mrs. Yarnell."

"And?"

"Before I could answer, the cop came with his siren going."

"No."

"Yup. I asked the officer what was wrong."

"He said we had to move."

"I told him we were on public property, and we had a right to be there."

"He said he had received a complaint we were harassing people."

"The lady called him Darnell, and said we weren't harassing her but just talking to her," Seth said.

"He threatened to arrest us and impound our camera," Greg said. "I asked him for his name and badge number."

"So, these people called me and Brossner to complain. Interesting," Kim said. "Seems people are touchy about this."

"Can they try to stop our story?" Marcie said.

"That goes under the freedom of the press," Greg said.

Marcie nodded.

"We'll handle it if it comes to that," Kim said.

"Now we have to narrow down all our information into an informative and entertaining piece," Marcie said.

"Small task," Greg said with a shrug. He had been swaying in a swivel chair bordering the table. "You know, when you first mentioned this piece, I thought it would be easy. Not so much."

26

April

The anesthesiologist said, "Count backward from 10, April."
 10 -9...
 April was running on the field. Her eyes were on the ball as her feet pounded the grass. The stick was clutched firmly in her fingers. A girl was glaring at her when she looked up. Her tongue adjusted her mouthpiece. The referee blew the whistle, and April passed the ball to Madison. Madison dribbled the ball and flicked it over to April. April, running to catch up to the ball, caught it and continued dribbling down the field. Her leg muscles were pumping, and her breath was quickening. An opposing team member hit her stick to get the ball. April's forearms tingled from the hit. April flicked the ball to Madison. Her breath steadied. Another player hit April from the side, and April fell forward, hitting the ground hard. Her body was pressed against the hard surface. She spit out some grime.*

She was walking with Madison and Ashley after the game. They were sweaty. "I could wring out my shirt," April said.
 "Your goal was awesome, April."
 "Ashley, why didn't the coach put you in today?"
 Ashley shrugged.
 "Wittenberg's coach was here today, and coach knew it."
 April stopped. "Wait. we were all going to Miami."
 "Not if you can't play. You need to run, April."
 Suddenly, she was in the stands sitting with her English teacher.
 "I'm not sure what I want to do for my extended essay, Mrs. Winslow. Could I do it on sports injuries? Media?"

"Why would you want to do it on sports injuries? Wouldn't that be painful for you?"
"Well, its due tomorrow."
A boy she didn't know sat down. "Hi, want to go to prom?"
"I don't know you."
"So? We can still go. I'll help you with your essay, then you can go."

***

"April, would you like some ice chips?"

April tried to wake up to answer. She was thirsty. Her eyes were heavy. She tried to focus on her blurry dad at the end of her bed. He was smiling. Her eyelids were heavy. Shifting her gaze, she attempted to concentrate on her mom. "Yes, please."

Her eyes drooped closed. Cold ice chips were being pressed against her lips. She opened her mouth and the ice chips slipped in on her tongue. She sucked on the ice as the cool, melted water slipped down her throat.

"Dr. Khumalo said everything went according to plan. The bullet is out. Now rest easy." She heard her father say.

She slipped into a dreamless sleep.
***

April woke to find her dad uncomfortably napping in the chair beside her bed. His head rested on his hand, and his long legs were crossed. A news program played on the television. The door of her room opened. "Hi, April. I'm in just to check your IV and take your temperature."

April looked at the whiteboard in her room. This nurse's name was Bonnie.

"Can I raise my bed?"

She looked at the IV in April's hand and followed it to the bag above April's head. It was almost empty.

"That's something I can do for you. "

She typed into the iPad she had with her. With April's forehead as the target, she used the digital thermometer to record and enter data. Moving to the other side of the bed, she took April's blood pressure. "Okay, that's it for now," Bonnie said. "Can I get you anything?" She looked down at her screen. "How about some jello or broth?"

April said, "No, but thanks."

As Bonnie turned to leave, April reached under her covers and moved her left leg slightly to the side. She tried to move her right leg. "Bonnie, are my toes moving on my right side? I can't feel them."

Bonnie moved to the right side of the bed and pulled up the blanket and sheet. "No, April. They aren't moving."

April turned to her dad. "Dad, Dad."

Malaki woke. He blinked his eyes a few times. His gaze turned to April, and he sat forward. "You're awake. How do you feel?"

"Dad, I can't move my toes."

He looked at Bonnie, who stood at the foot of April's bed. Shaking the arm he had been leaning on, he said, "April, it won't happen right away. I'm sure there's swelling at the sight of where the bullet was."

He nodded to Bonnie. She nodded back and left.

April sighed.

"I know. But it will take some time."

April looked down at her hands. A tear ran down her cheek. She wiped it away. "I just thought…"

He stood and sat on the bed, facing his daughter. "Patience is hard to have right now. But the doctor said everything went according to plan. They'll assess everything, and Eric and Tessa will be back to help you. You'll be back home in a day or so."

"How long will it be before I can return to school?"

"As soon as next week."

"Well, there's that."

"You okay? I should go back to the lab. Your mom will be here tonight."

He kissed her on the head and stood. April said, "Okay, Dad. I'll see you later."

***

Dr. Khumalo told her she would start PT the following day, and Eric got her at ten in the morning. After massaging and exercising her right leg, he asked her to move her toes. She couldn't.

"Guess it will take some more time, but let's keep the left one moving. Shall we?"

Instead of starting the routine, April sat leaning on her

hands, her legs forward. Eric sat back on his heels. "What's wrong?"

"Why didn't you and Tessa tell me this was hopeless?"

"What is?"

"Everything we've been doing."

April folded her arms as she leaned forward. He wrapped a blue band around his hand, then said, "April, what makes you think what we're doing is hopeless?"

"I thought you guys said my legs would be fine after the operation."

"April, your body is still healing. The operation was invasive. The tissues around the nerves are swollen."

"Then what?"

"We wait and see. The tests look positive."

Sighing, April said, "I don't see how I'll dance at my prom if anyone asks me."

"When's the prom?"

"In about two months."

Eric looked off to the left. "Well, I can't say positively we'll have you up on your dancing feet by then, but April, see these muscles in your legs? There are five major muscles. Do you know why we work your glutes? Because everything is connected. When you sit as you have been, your legs are not getting a lot of exercise or stimulation. We've been working both sides, but you'll be most effective when moving your legs yourself. I can't guess what timetable your muscles and tendons are on, but we will keep them alive and work them so that you're strong enough to use them when they're ready. It's going to take a lot of work. Tessa and I will work with you until you're up and walking."

"Up and running is what people say."

"Let's concentrate on walking. I'm not going to lie to you or baby you. Come on. Let's get started. What do you say?"

***

April was back at school the next week, as her dad predicted. The buzz about the prom was in full swing. The theme had already been chosen. "Fire and Ice," April pictured herself in a "Catching Fire" Katniss dress or an ice blue Elsalike dress. Of course, she always pictured herself dancing at the prom. The stresses of wanting to go to prom, deciding on her extended essay subject, working on other projects, plus physical therapy caused April to have headaches.

"Why don't you interview Ms. Reynolds, April, for the Media and Its Effects? She might help you narrow down the topic a bit, as Mrs. Winslow suggested.

April realized her mom was trying to help, but she couldn't motivate herself. Other projects were easier because others were helping. The deadline for declaring her essay subject loomed. "Mrs. Reynolds, this is April Simmons. You brought me some things from Channel 10."

"Of course, I remember you, April. What can I do for you?"

"I have a research project for my IB ELA 2 class, and I would like to interview you about the effects of the media on the global society."

"Wow. That's a broad topic."

"I don't know how to narrow it down."

"How about brainstorming what interest you may have? Do you want to research about the effects on children? Politics? Styles of clothing?"

April laughed. "This is hard."

"I'm a pro. My daughter and I collaborated on multiple school projects.

"Researching something that matters is important to me."

"Hm. I'm working on a documentary about how cultures can encourage bullying."

"You are?"

"My reporter and I are outlining it."

"That's pretty current, isn't it?"

"We should talk more about it, but I have to leave for a meeting."

"Okay, thanks. I'd like that."

As Marcie hung up, she wondered if that was the best thing to have suggested. She, Greg, and Kim have continued to discuss how to approach it. They ran a lot by the legal team, and no one thought there would be problems if they did it correctly. April seemed so low about what topic to choose for her project that she blurted out the idea.

***

Her mom's eyebrows raised when April told her she called Mrs. Reynolds. "That's great, honey. What did she say?"

"She and her reporter are working on a documentary about bullying. That would be a good topic.

"Good for you, April. Is that something you would be interested in doing?"

"It's current. You hear about cyberbullying all the time."

"True. Does bullying happen in other countries? Wouldn't you need to add that to make it global?"

April laughed. "Have you talked to Mrs. Winslow?"

Her mom colored. "Well. The subject came up at the last parent-teacher conference.

"It's okay, Mom."

"Why don't you discuss it Mrs. Winslow?"

"I will."

***

At work the next day, Adele took a minute to call Marcie. "Mrs. Reynolds, this is Adele Simmons, April's mom."

"Hi, Mrs. Simmons."

"I wanted to thank you for helping April. She has been so down. She perked up yesterday after she talked to you."

"I'm glad to hear that."

"I have a favor to ask."

"What do you need?"

"April told me you were working on a project about bullying."

Marcie paused. "Yes."

"Could April help you somehow? She needs something to make her feel... She needs something exciting. Something positive."

"Hm. Why don't April and I talk and see what we can do?"

"That would be great, thank you."

Marcie sat back in her chair at the station, wondering the feasibility of this working.

Marcie called Gabz, administrative assistant to Kim

Wolford, Executive News Producer/Community Relations Manager. for Channel Ten. "Gabz, I need to propose something to Kim. Does she have any time to meet with me?"

"Let's see. Can you run up now? She has about a fifteen-minute breather."

"I'll be right up."

Kim was sitting at her desk when Marcie knocked. Looking up, Kim said, "Problem, proposal, or social call?"

"Proposal. I need to brainstorm an idea with you that might be good public relations."

"I don't care. I just want to get from behind this desk."

Kim stood and came around to where Marcie was standing. "Oh, that's better. Mind if we stand while we talk?"

"No problem. Do you remember the incident concerning the senior who was shot in Springridge?"

Kim stretched her neck and shoulders, moving her head from side to side. "Yes, it's the basis for the documentary."

"She was paralyzed from the waist down."

"Yes, the shooter's in prison."

"Right. Yes. I received a call from the girl's mother."

"Fundraiser?"

"No, something more unusual."

"Okay."

"She's working on a complicated essay. She is in an International Baccalaureate program. I want to involve her as a researcher on the project."

"Hm. Remind me about the program."

"It's rigorous. April will need to look at bullying from both a world and domestic point of view. It fits. This could be the missing piece. We examine how a culture can create and perpetuate bullying using Springridge as a microcosm. April will look at other cultures."

"Is this what her mother called you about?"

"April has had a bad time of it. She's down, and her mother thought if we could involve her, it might lift her spirits."

"The parents would have to be informed what you and Greg are doing and give permission."

"Kim, she still can't walk. She would research, give an interview, and have a credit at the end.

"Would you bring her here at the station? That might raise

her spirits a bit."
    "What a good idea."
    "As if you didn't consider that. Tell Greg not to scare her."
    Marcie laughed. "I'll tell him not to."

27

Principal Trundle

It took Marcie several calls to schedule Principal Trundle of Springridge High School for an interview. She began by calling the high school, and Trundle's secretary said she had to start with the Superintendent. She called the Board of Education office, and she was referred to the Public Relations office. The Public Relations Officer told her there was some mistake and that she indeed had to talk to the Superintendent. He was out visiting a school, so she left a message.

She waited for three days and called back. "This is Superintendent Riedel's office. Pam Jones speaking."

"Hi. Ms. Jones. This is Marcie Reynolds from WCMS TV News. I called the other day to speak to Superintendent Riedel."

"What is this in relation to?"

"I called the other day. I would like to speak to Principal Trundle about one tradition of the Springridge High School students."

"Why are you calling here?"

"Because the secretary at the high school told me, I am required to get permission first from Superintendent Riedel."

"Oh, I see. Let me check with the Superintendent."

Marcie was placed on hold. After listening to brain-numbing music for five minutes, Ms. Jones returned. "Mrs. Reynolds, the Superintendent said the school district's policy is not to sanction any senior traditions or pranks. Thank you for calling."

"Wait. Are you saying I tell a reporter that he has permission

116

to talk to the principal or not?"

"There's no reason. We don't approve of those traditions."

"Ms. Jones, we are going to do a news documentary on the incident that took place on Halloween last year. Would the superintendent prefer my reporter to say that the Springridge School System would not cooperate with us and seemed to have something to hide and that you don't sanction any traditions the high school has, including what? Prom? Graduation? And don't hang up on me, or I will also have that reported."

"Hold on, please."

"Superintendent Riedel."

"Superintendent Riedel, hello. I am Marcie Reynolds, Investigator Producer at Channel 10 News."

"How can I help you?"

"I would like you to allow us to interview Principal Trundle about the senior tradition concerning the Ghost House."

"We don't sanction the senior tradition at the Ghost House."

"Yes, but one of your seniors is now trying to learn to walk again because it has been a ritual for many years. We are looking into how this situation was instigated."

"Why?"

"Why, what?"

"Why would you look into something that happened in Springridge?"

"Springridge is a microcosm of a larger city like Columbus. Studies show that the rate of bullying goes beyond the confines of the environment of a school. We're curious to find what elements exist in communities that create an atmosphere that makes it okay for bullying, cyberbullying, road rage, and bullying in the workplace. It's been proven that it affects cognitive and non-cognitive aspects of people."

"You're not looking to blame the school for what happened in October?"

"No, we're not."

"I'll let Principal Trundle know it is okay to grant an interview with your reporter."

"Thank you."

As Marcie hung up, she turned in her chair to find Greg at her office's door.

"Wow. Cognitive, non-cognitive. I'm impressed."

Marcie shrugged one shoulder as she typed. "I've been reading about bullying. It seems it's worldwide."

"You can help April in her research."

"Yes, well. She only has a little time to do her essay. But I also had a feeling the Superintendent wouldn't let you interview the principal if we were going to put the blame on the school. I'm booking your interview for early next week. It's my next call."

Trundle: Welcome to Springridge High School.

Greg: Thanks; our producer said you didn't want to sit in your office for this interview. You wanted to show us around.

Trundle: The school environment is outside my office. It's in the hallways and classrooms of the school.

Greg nodded. "Okay, let's do a tour."

Trundle: I don't have to remind you that students cannot be in your video without permission from their parents.

Greg said. "You just did."

They started in the main hallway, where there were signs of what the school had done to improve its environment. The school colors were red and blue. But a person didn't see an excessive amount of red. The school walls were light blue. The school lockers were a deep blue. Graphics on the walls included the scarlet color and burgundy and cream. The graphics and signs included steps to take care of the school, Be Kind, and Eleanor Roosevelt quotes, *"You must do the thing you think you cannot do."* and *"No one can make you feel inferior without your consent."*

They stopped in the school's commons, where Trundle and Greg sat. Seth set up the camera to focus on the principal. They could do cutaways later.

Greg: Let's talk about seniors and their traditions.

Trundle: Yes. That. I've been here seven years, and I've seen one or two come and go.

Greg: But there was one.

Trundle: Yes.

Greg: The Ghost House, where kids were knocking on the doors and windows of the man's house, sometimes egging it, sometimes soaping or waxing the windows. Harassing the guy who lived there.

Trundle: First, let me say it was never sanctioned by the school or the school system. According to people I asked, it began a long time ago. Some of the students' parents did it in their day.

Greg: Long time.

Trundle: Yes, a long time.

Greg: Why do you suppose?

Trundle: Wish I knew. It seems individuals go after someone different or, in their eyes, weaker. Our program here at Springridge assists students when they are being bullied. The librarians invite students who are chronically picked on to work with them as aides. That's been going on for a long time. The counselors and I offer an open door to students and parents who want to report cyberbullying, and we counsel both sides of cyberbullying. Yes, there are consequences, but we want to get to the root of the problem. Sometimes it is bullying. Other times, it may be revenge or jealousy.

Greg: What do you suggest for parents?

Trundle: Listen for what your kids are doing. Don't elevate a squabble. Ask questions.

Greg: Do you think the parents of the kids harassing Ben Franklin realized what they were doing?

Trundle: I can't say. I don't know.

28

April's Dad Dr. Malaki Simmons

Greg had asked Dr. Simmons if he preferred to be interviewed at his office or home. He preferred his office. Greg and Seth were requested to go to a back door connected to his office because it would avoid any labs and waiting areas involving patients. Seth brought his camera and light kit. When a man wearing scrubs answered their knock, his eyes widened when he saw the camera and Seth. "Are you sure you are in the right place?" He asked.

"I wrote down specifically where Dr. Simmons said we should go," said Greg.

"Okay then, I will check with him. Will you wait here?"

"Okay."

"Strange," Seth said.

Greg nodded his agreement. He took several steps back and checked his notebook in his back pocket. After a few minutes, he looked at his watch. Seth readjusted his camera on his shoulder.

The door opened again, and the man said, "He said I'm to take you directly to his office."

"That will be fine," Greg said. "Want me to carry that?" He pointed to the light kit.

"Yeah, thanks," said Seth.

The attendant escorted them down several white halls. Every single hall door had been shut. Greg noted many of the doors had labels identifying them as labs. When their escort paused and opened a door, he stepped back and allowed Greg and Seth to enter. He turned to leave and shut the door.

Greg said, "If they didn't want us to see anything, why have us come in the back door?"

Seth said, "Maybe the waiting rooms are in the front."

Greg stuck out his bottom lip and nodded. "Well, let's get on with this."

Seth got out his light meter and opened the light kit.

Dr. Simmons came in and shook hands with both men. Dr. Simmons said, "Before we start, I just want to say I hope the guy never gets out. I believe he should have been charged with attempted murder."

Greg nodded. "Well, sir, I can understand your anger. How about we have you sitting in this chair?"

"I prefer behind my desk."

"Seth, can you light him there?"

Seth moved the lights to allow Dr. Simmons to sit where he wanted. "Can do, Greg."

"Dr. Simmons, Seth here will put a microphone on you. It will be easy with your lab coat. I'll ask you a few things so he can get a sound check, and then we'll start."

Dr. Simmons walked to sit behind his desk. Seth stopped him to place a lavaliere mike on his coat.

"How's April doing?" Greg asked.

"She's doing as well as expected. I hear she's been in touch with a Marcie Reynolds at your station."

"Yes, in fact, she will be helping with this documentary we're putting together. Ms. Reynolds is pleased to have her input."

"I just don't want you to take advantage of her."

"How would we do that, sir?"

"You guys could have her feeling sorry for the guy who shot her. Who knows?"

"Got your sound check, Seth?"

Seth nodded.

Greg: "It's been almost six months since your daughter experienced the unfortunate incident involving Ben Franklin.

Dr. Simmons: We received a call from Madison and Ashley that April was taken to the hospital. I answered the phone and asked them what happened. They said she had been shot.

When we arrived at the hospital emergency, the doctor was waiting for an MRI to see where the bullet had lodged.

Greg: How did April appear at that point?

Dr. Simmons: She expressed concern regarding her inability to move her legs and her friends' well-being. The staff had stemmed the bleeding at this point. Once the MRI had been completed, a police officer arrived, and April related to us what had transpired.

Greg: That she was shot and how it happened?

Dr. Simmons: Yes.

Greg: Were you aware the girls planned a senior prank that night?

Dr. Simmons: (hesitating) We knew of the tradition.

Greg: Can you explain what you thought the tradition was?

Dr. Simmons: The girls mentioned that there is a tradition of taking selfies at this guy's house. Several of their friends had already done it, and they wanted to do it too. We believed it would cause no one harm since it was Halloween and kids were going door to door. (He shrugged.)

Greg: Did you realize it involved knocking on his door and windows?

Dr. Simmons: (shifting in his seat) No.

Greg: Were you aware that his house had been vandalized in the past for this tradition?

Dr. Simmons: No.

Greg: Did you or your wife check into this tradition before you let April and her friends take part in it?

Dr. Simmons: No, Mr. Stanton, we didn't. We took the girls' word that they would take a selfie at his house. That's all.

Greg: (nodding) Did you have any idea how long this tradition has been taking place?

Dr. Simmons: Madison said the tradition had been going on for a long time.

Greg: Yes, sir, she was correct. The tradition has been going on since Franklin experienced bullying in high school.

Dr. Simmons: If the guy felt so bothered by it, why didn't he leave that night? Why didn't he call the police? Why didn't he move?

Greg: Didn't you say the girls told you several of their friends had already done it, and they wanted to do it, too?

Halloween was one of many nights he had to put up with this tradition.

Dr. Simmons: I guess not, but did you look at that house? It was an eyesore. The city should have been citing him to cut down the bushes and cut his grass. He contributed to the mischief.

Greg: The court records say Franklin had to pay restitution.

Dr. Simmons: Yes, we forced him to help with the doctors and hospital bills, and physical therapy.

Greg: Insurance doesn't pay for everything.

Dr. Simmons: My wife and I are grateful for what it pays and the help of all the doctors and physical therapists. But you know. April wanted to play Field Hockey in college. She wanted to go to the same schools as her friends. That guy took that away from her. Now she can't play Field Hockey ever again. She can attend the same school, but sitting on the sidelines while they play would be hard.

Greg: What do you think she'll do?

Dr. Simmons: She is determined to walk again. My wife and I are proud of her. Whether she even goes away to school or stays here at Midtown, we are hoping she has those choices to make.

Greg: Thank you, Dr. Simmons, for talking to us. Do you have anything you want to add?

Dr. Simmons: No. Thank you, gentlemen, for coming.

29

April

April arrived at physical therapy early. She had a strenuous day in her morning classes. She declared her research topic and showed her initial outline to Mrs. Winslow. Her teacher thought she had a lot more work to do. She believed April's sources were adequate, but she needed to strengthen her thesis and provide a better outline. She reminded April that deadline to complete for IB coursework was in one month. April knew to have credit for the course, she needed to finish it on time.

Eric walked over to her after finishing with another patient. "Hey, how's it going?"

April looked up at him and said, "Not good."

"Sorry to hear about that, but I'm changing things up today. Come on."

He walked behind her and pushed her toward the exit. "Where are we going?"

"I guess you'll see."

He pushed her down two long halls to another workout area, April observed more parallel bars, devices that looked like stand-up wheelchairs, and another set of parallel bars with a device of some sort hanging by it. "It's time you have the experience of walking again. Let's go."

He pushed her toward the hanging device by the parallel bars. "April, this apparatus suspends you while we stabilize your hips and legs as you learn to walk naturally again. Come on, let's start by strapping you in."

He placed the straps around April's body first. "When we get this on and secure, we'll put this strap under you."

April helped him adjust the straps and buckles so they were comfortable. "Tessa will be here to help you simulate walking. She will be behind you, and I will be in front. Here she is."

"April, hi. I hope I didn't keep you waiting."

"No, you're good."

"Okay, April. Ready? I'm going to get you up on your feet."

Eric stepped away. Tessa took her place behind April. "Okay, April. I'll tell you when to boost yourself with your arms out of your seat. Tessa will guide you between the bars. Reach forward for the bars to stabilize yourself."

Tessa braked her chair. April sensed the straps tightening. "Now April. Boost yourself!"

April reached back with her hands and grasped the armrests of her chair. She pushed herself out of the chair and Eric pulled cables to help her while Tessa guided her hips between the bars. April grabbed the bars as she rose further from her chair. April laughed and could hardly breathe. "Are the straps too tight?" Eric asked.

"No! I'm good."

April looked down at her legs dangling in the space between the apparatus. "I'm going to settle you now. Look up, keep your chin parallel to the floor."

She continued to look down and saw her feet slowly settle on the floor. Eric came in front of her and sat on a short stool with wheels. "Okay, April, we are going to go turtle speed. You are going to move your legs from your hips. Tessa and I will guide your legs to help you walk. We're going to get some blood flowing, baby!"

April laughed. Eric bent her knees. Tessa stabilized her hips. April pushed her left hip as her one knee and foot moved forward, and then she observed her other knee and foot catch up. She pulled forward with her arms.

"Oh, God. This is so weird!" April yelled and laughed.

"Put your head up, April. It keeps your body in line."

The next ten minutes flew by. April concentrated on moving her hips and legs. She was certain she felt parts of her left foot touch the floor. Despite the numbness of her right leg, she detected movement. When she reached the end of the bars, Tessa and Eric turned her around and she walked back.

Eric and Tessa carefully lowered her into her wheelchair and out of the device. "Eric and Tessa, it felt so good to stand."

Back in their usual workout room, they were going through her routine, when Eric jerked his face up and met April's gaze. "April, did you feel your toe move?"

"On my left foot. Sure."

"No, you're right."

"No."

"Can you try to move it?"

April concentrated on her right big toe. She shook her head. Then it moved. April raised her eyebrows, and she grinned at Eric. "Did you see that?"

"I did."

He reached over and cupped her toes and massaged them. "I still can't feel that."

"But it moved. Maybe the nerves sending messages are making it to your brain again."

April beamed.

***

The next day at school, April wheeled into her Psychology class. Because she arrived early, no one else was there. An enormous poster with crudely drawn ice cubes and campfires and the words, "April, Will you go to Prom with me?" decorated the back wall. April stared at it. She drew her chair closer to it to see if it was signed. It wasn't. She turned her chair around, and Payton, the boy she had been working with on a project, stood with several carnations. Behind him stood her entire class and Mr. Mischal, her teacher. April's face grew hot. She raised her hands to her face. "Oh my God, Payton," she said.

He walked to her and gave her the flowers. April looked up at him and smiled, "Yes. I'd love to go to prom with you."

Everyone applauded.

In the car on the way home, April texted her mom. "Payton asked me to prom today!"

Her mom texted back. "Great. Let's go shopping."

***

April fell in love with the first dress she saw. A deep apricot A-line boat neck illusion tea-length chiffon prom dress with prism beading sparkling on the bodice decorated a manikin. April felt uncomfortable trying it on at the store, but she decided she needed to try it. She pushed herself into the large room with a try fold mirror. She pulled her tee shirt over her head. Her mom told her to lift her arms and Pam, the lady who helped them, and her mom floated the dress around her. Pam told her mom to wait a minute. She came back with another woman. "April needs to see this dress standing up."

"April, do you think you can do it?" Adele asked.

April bit her lower lip. "Let's try."

April moved her chair in front of the mirror. "Put the brake on, Mom." Adele snapped the brake on and flipped up the foot pieces. Pam and the other lady named Claire helped April as she pushed herself from the chair. "Hold me. I can't stand on my own, yet." April told the ladies.

As April stood between the women holding her up, her mom zipped the dress. April looked at her standing image. She held her head high and smiled. She looked to her left and right to noticed both women holding her in tears. Over her shoulder, her mom smiled at her daughter. Her mom asked if she wanted to look at any other dresses. "No, I think this one will be fine," April said.

As April settled back into her chair, Claire brought her soft leather shoes colored in a deep yellow.

"Mom, what if we ordered Payton a yellow rose tipped in apricot as a boutonniere?"

"I'll call tomorrow," her mom said.

April nodded, knowing her mom wanted to participate in the preparation.

Prom text messages zoomed back and forth between April and Ashley. A boy in Ashley's IB English Lit. class asked her to prom. The girls asked their dates if they could go together to dinner. The guys were fine with it. Another foursome joined them to form a group of eight. They brainstormed how they would all go together and included April's wheelchair. Hilarious ideas were suggested, such as attaching it to the top of a limo or having an Uber deliver it to the restaurant and prom. They decided two couples would drive, and Payton would put the wheelchair in the back of his mother's SUV.

Madison, engrossed in the softball season, was going to the prom with a baseball player she liked for a long time. When Ashley and April texted her to include her in their planning, she ignored their texts or answered with "Can't talk now." Ashley and April heard later Madison joined the baseball/softball group.

A week before the big day, the announcements for prom king and queen nominations took place. There was a total of four girls and four boys on the court. Madison and April received nominations. Madison's date made it onto the list for the boys, but Payton did not. The excitement for the juniors and seniors ratcheted up. Teachers held back on assignments for upper-class students, recognizing it as a lost cause. They were secretly relieved the prom occurred so early in the spring. Girls who had not been asked planned to join in the fun together. Boys who did not ask anyone feigned disinterest.

Ashley texted April, who had just returned home from physical therapy. *Did you see this?* She had copied a text from another girl in the group.

April is on the court because everyone pities her. Vote for Madison.

Where did you get this?

Lucie sent it to me. WTF What should we do?

Nothing. I'm just glad I'm going.

Are you sure?

Yes. I don't care.

Two days later, the message was repeated on Instagram. The Friday before prom, two softball players placed a video on TikTok. It featured an earlier video of April walking in the hall. A message was typed in, "She's faking."

April showed it to her mom when she came home. "Do you want me to call the principal, April? This is wrong."

"No, mom. I'm just glad I'm going."

When Adele told April's dad later in the evening, she said, "Malaki, I am ashamed to say I was angrier than April. This whole incident has made her become so much more mature."

***

Dinner was at a restaurant where April had never been before. It was close to the prom venue and served Italian food. Payton had asked Dr. Simmons how to handle April's chair, which made Malaki happy. Payton even called the restaurant to ensure they had a spot ready for April so they didn't have to wait for a place to be created.

Getting in and out of the car could have been awkward, but when Payton, who was a foot taller than April, leaned over to let her put her arms around his neck, they both started laughing. He stood up, swung her around, and gently lowered her in her chair. Ashley and her date walked up to keep April company as he drove to park the SUV. He steered her into the restaurant, and the server showed them to a private area where April's chair fit comfortably.

The prom was at the Franklin Park Conservatory in Columbus. Their party of eight all entered the venue together. Because April was with them, they all piled into the elevator, allowing them to avoid the line formed by the stairs leading to the prom location. Payton pushed her through an exhibit where they enjoyed bonsai trees and orchids. A tropical rainforest area with waterfalls was April's favorite. Pausing in the Palm House, they sat in a wrought iron gazebo, talking about nothing in particular. They returned to the area where the disc jockey provided the music for dancing. The small dance floor was crowded, but it suited April and Payton. Surrounding the dance floor were white tables and chairs, so April and Payton were close to the music and action. During the song YMCA, Payton started making the dance moves as he remained sitting. April's eyebrows went up, and she grinned at him. She joined him, laughing. From then on, they danced, with Payton even spinning her around as she sat in her chair.

The court nominees came up by the DJ right before ten o'clock. The organizing teacher noticed Madison was absent when the girls posed around April for the photographer. She asked the DJ to announce Madison's name. He even stopped the music once to announce her name again. A chaperone came back and whispered to the teacher. April watched the teacher move into the crowd of kids. Ten minutes later, she returned and permitted the DJ to go ahead and announce the Homecoming court. The king was Madison's date. The queen was announced as Madison. But she didn't appear. Kids were whispering she was in the restroom being sick. Her parents had to be called to take her home. Madison's date found another girl to dance the King and Queen dance. April and Payton joined them on the dance floor. Waiting in the parking lot afterwards as Payton went to retrieve his car, April sighed with contentment.

30

Ben

Ben's habit was to stay in his cell and read, but lately, he preferred sitting in the open area. Terry believed it indicated that possibly Ben was becoming more secure. Rick came up to Ben and said Terry had good news for him.

Together, they walked to Terry's office. "Hey, both of you, come in."

Ben made his way to his regular seat. Terry came around his desk and stood with Rick. "Ben, we can get you into the Kent State Library Science program."

"Okay, does that mean we don't get a computer in the library?"

"I don't get what you mean, Ben."

"Am I going to Kent?"

"No. It means we'll get the computer in the library, and you can take courses online to Kent and work with the Dayton Library System."

"Oh, okay. When?"

"That's what I wanted to show you. Administration has installed the computer in the library, and it's waiting for you."

Ben stood immediately and headed for the door. Rick and Terry laughed. "I guess he didn't need an escort. Let's go join him," Terry said.

They entered the library to find Ben sitting at the desk, powering up the computer. "It's just a Dell, but that's okay. It's locked down; that's good," Ben said to no one. "Do I have a login?"

"Yes, here." Terry handed Ben a Post-it note.

Ben nodded and quickly logged on to the computer. "It has Microsoft, and you can log into the Dayton Library and Kent State. It's connected to the system here at the prison, so they will detect if you go into any other websites. There's also a program for you to record any of the books we have here. It shouldn't take you long to add what we have. It will be your job to get books that might interest the other prisoners or take requests that you can borrow from the Dayton library. The list must be approved by the warden."

"Okay."

"Ben, do you understand that the warden has to approve any books requested by the inmates?" Rick asked.

Ben didn't seem to be listening. He was looking at the programs on the computer.

"Ben," Terry said. "Listen. What you will do until we can figure out another way. If an inmate requests a book, you will write a note to the warden and leave it with me. I will take it to the warden's secretary, and she'll take it from there."

"Ben", Rick said.

"I heard you. I'll take the request to Terry, and he will take it from there."

Terry and Rick looked at each other.

Ben stood and walked to the bookshelf to his left. He started taking the books down and piling them on the desk.

"I guess he wants to get to work," Rick said.

Terry and Rick turned and left the library.

***

Ben had entered at least twenty books when he noticed it was lunchtime. After lunch, he was scheduled to weed in the garden area. Walking down the corridor, he noticed Keno coming in the opposite direction. He looked around to duck into an open door, but they were all closed. He had nowhere to go.

Keno was smiling at Ben when he got close to him. "Hey, it's the brain kid,"

"Why did you call me that?" Ben averted his eyes.

"I hear you're always reading."

Keno stooped to get in Ben's face. "Why don't you look at me?"

Ben moved to the left of him to get around him. Keno sidestepped in front of him. Ben moved to the right, and Keno blocked him. He gripped Ben's arm and raised his fist to his face. "I said, why don't you look at me?"

Ben tried to pull away from him, but Keno squeezed tighter. He grabbed Ben's face and brought it around to his. "Don't you like how I look?"

Keno was smiling. Ben said, "Let go!"

"Okay, that's enough." A guard came down the hall behind both men.

"No problem. I was just trying to make a friend," Keno said.

He let Ben free and swaggered down the hall. Ben stood still and rubbed his arm. "You better hurry if you are going to eat lunch," the guard said.

***

Ben was getting dressed after a shower when Brody asked him where the bruise on his arm came from.

Ben shrugged. "You can see the fingerprints on you," Brody stared at him. "Okay, you're coming with me."

"I gotta go to the library."

"No, you're not. I said you're coming with me."

Brody led Ben to the area outside where the men were lifting weights and doing Tai Chi. Chee was leading. Brody and Ben waited until Chee completed the class.

"Chee, Ben here needs your help."

"Keno," was all Chee said.

"Yup."

"Okay, Ben. I'm going to teach you some things."

They left there and got the okay from a guard to go to an area that looked more like a wrestling room. Chee pulled out a mat. "Ben, have you ever taken a defense class like Jiu-Jitsu?"

"I've read about it and seen pictures."

"Okay, well, now you will learn how you will do it."

***

Rick made a habit of meeting Ben for breakfast. Most of the time, they talked about books Ben had examined or read. Sometimes, Rick would tell him how he planned to get a job helping ex-cons adjust to outside life and to persuade people to employ former inmates. Ben gave him ideas of places inmates could go, like movie places. He even told Rick they could be Uber drivers like Brody wanted. Today, after they were settled and eating. Ben said, "I like the new computer."

"That's great, Ben."

"Did you know there are four ways to get out of hold?"

Rick's face registered confusion. "What kind of hold? I didn't realize there's a hold on a computer."

"When someone holds your arm."

"No, I didn't. How did you find that out?"

"Chee and Brody."

"Somehow, that should explain that. You want to tell me?"

"Brody and Chee said I need to learn how to handle bullies. They're teaching me."

"Hmph." Rick nodded his head. "Sounds reasonable. Okay, Ben. I have something I need to tell you."

Ben kept on eating. "Ben, my time is up. I'm going to be getting out."

Ben stopped with his fork in midair. "Is Terry leaving too?"

"No, no. Ben, I hope to get back to see how you're doing. If you are up for parole in three years, I'll be here to give a character reference. I'll be leaving in a week. I'll see you before I get out. I just wanted to let you know."

"Okay, Rick."

Rick told Terry he thought Ben would be fine after he left. He didn't sense any concern.

***

After Rick left the prison, Ben didn't eat breakfast. He stayed in his cell until it was time for lunch or the gardens. Terry brought him in the day after Rick left, but Ben hardly said anything. He let him go back to his cell after twenty minutes.

Brody tried to get him to take more lessons from Chee. He

even asked him to go to the library to find a book for him. All Ben said was, "You don't like to read."

It took Ben about a week to adjust to Rick not being there to talk. He tried to tell Brody about the books he wanted to bring in or about a lesson he learned. These were all the things Ben used to talk to Rick about. But he quit when Brody couldn't respond. All he said was, "That's great, Ben."

Ben asked for an appointment with Terry.

Terry responded immediately and asked a guard to have Ben come in after he returned from the garden. "I have to go to lunch," Ben said.

"I'll tell him you said that. But I suggest you go now."

As the guard led the way, a guy elbowed Ben in the gut as they passed a crew coming in from the outside yards. Ben folded to the floor. The guard backtracked to Ben. After ensuring he was okay, he looked at the crew as they continued to file by. No one looked like they had done anything. The guard helped Ben stand.

The guard knocked on the door when they got to Terry's office. Ben was still rubbing his stomach when he entered. He made a beeline for the chair and slouched.

Terry, as was the custom, looked up to observe Ben. "Ben, what happened?

"A guy elbowed me."

Terry nodded, stood, and sat on the corner of his desk. He wanted to give Ben space. "Do you know who it was?"

Ben shook his head no. "Have you seen him before?"

"I'm not sure. Maybe in the rec area. It happened kinda fast."

"Ben, we need to talk about how you react when someone bullies you."

Ben folded his arms. "It used to happen all the time."

"In school?"

Ben nodded. "Can you tell me about it?"

"They called me Benny or Stupid."

"Go on."

"My mom would tell me I wasn't stupid and I shouldn't care what they call me. When I was little, the boys would take my book bag, throw my books in the trash, and stomp on my lunch. I had to get glasses. One kid would smear them when he came up to me or come up behind me and knock them off my face. One time, a big kid had me up against the lockers. I pushed him away, but then he slapped my face, saying, 'What's wrong, Benny? Can't you walk to school by yourself?'"

"How old were you?"

"Twelve."

"Your mom walked you to school? To stop the bullies? Weren't there any other kids around?"

"They wouldn't walk with me. My mom would yell at the kids, or she would have Harry with her. He'd squawk and hiss."

"Who was Harry?"

"Her parrot."

"Oh. I see."

"Tell me more about the kids at school."

"They were the reason Children's Services tried to take me away from my mom a couple of times."

"Come again?"

"My mom said when I was in fifth grade, I was a big boy who could walk to school alone. Kids took my coat."

"Once, I came to school without a winter coat on a very cold day. My teacher took me to the lost and found and got me one. The next day, I came again to school without a coat. I only had a tee shirt on. The teacher, school nurse, and counselor became concerned about how I was dressed. They tried to call the house, but I guess mom was having one of her spells and wouldn't answer the phone. "

"That's right, she had bipolar disorder."

"Two boys thought taking stuff while I was walking to school was funny. They threw my stuff over the cubbies at school so no one would know they did it. They told me they'd beat me up if I told.

"And?"

"Children's Services came to the house and questioned my mom."

"And she told them she had bought you a winter coat."

Ben nodded. "She went to school the next day and raised a stink. After the three women reported the information to children's services, the janitor found my two jackets and three sweaters behind the cubbies."

"Didn't you have any friends you could walk with?"

"No, the kids thought I was weird. In middle school, a new girl came to my class. Lucy was nice. She sat with me for a while until the boys and girls in my class wouldn't talk to her or made fun of her for sitting with me. Her parents came to school and complained. They finally removed her out of Bayberry and put her in St. Mary's school."

"Ben, how do you feel about that now?"

Ben sat quietly for a minute and said, "Mrs. Waxman told me I was smart, and the kids didn't understand how my brain worked. She made me feel better."

"She really helped you, didn't she?"

Still rubbing his abdomen, Ben nodded. "I have to go to lunch."

"Okay, let's look at this book list. I wrote some titles down I thought you could start requesting from Dayton."

Ben took the list from him. "Did the warden approve them?"

"I showed him these Monday, and he approved them."

"Ben, by the way, your class has started. Why don't you go to the library after lunch and get started on your class and this list."

"Okay." Ben stood and crossed to the door. After he left, Terry stayed sitting on his desk. He wondered how he was going to keep Ben safe.

31

April

While others traveled to Cedar Point the day after prom, April and Payton took in a Clippers Minor League baseball game. Like April, Payton loved baseball, but wasn't good at it. Huntington Park was chilly, but the sun provided the right atmosphere for the game. Eating hot dogs while cheering the Clippers on to win was perfect. Krash, one of the Clipper's mascots, even took a selfie with them.

After the prom, there were a lot of pictures on Instagram with Madison looking drunk with graphic crowns on her head. One photo showed her ashen face streaked with mascara and her eyes glassy. She was suspended from playing several softball games because the behavior violated the alcohol and drugs policy. Her coach pulled her into her office Monday after the prom to council her, but her teammates wouldn't talk to her all week.

April was looking at a busy May schedule. Graduation was the weekend of Memorial Day. She had her essay and several other projects to complete. Payton visited often and proved to be an added incentive for her to work on her essay. He would bring her home now that she stayed all day at school. They would spend extra hours working on research at April's home.

When she wasn't at school or researching, she was at physical therapy. She would strap into the apparatus that she called the Zombie Walker. "Ten more minutes," Eric said, looking up at her.

"It doesn't seem as tight as before," April said.

Eric had loosened the cables that held her to a standing

position. "Let's just try it."

April took three halting steps. She moved her left leg forward and then pull her right to meet it. On the third painstaking step, her left knee buckled and April caught herself on the side bars, taking her from her hands to her forearms. "Hold her," Eric said to Tessa.

Tessa grabbed the straps around April's waist. Eric tightened the cables. "Okay, let's finish the ten minutes.

"We're going to add the pool today. Did you bring your things?"

April said yes. After she changed into shorts and a top, Eric and Tessa pushed her to the natatorium. "April, this is Claudia and Sam. They specialize in helping people in the pool."

"Nice to meet you."

"Okay, April. We are going to shift you into this swing. By the way, can you swim?"

April laughed. "Now you think to ask me?"

"Well, I guess I figured you could."

Tessa said, "April, he asked your parents ages ago."

The swing lowered her into the tepid water. "Oh, this feels good," April said.

Claudia and Sam slipped into the pool next to her. "Okay, let's get her over to the treadmill."

"Treadmill?"

April looked at both therapists. Both smiled and nodded. Claudia helped her float over to the side of the pool where parallel bars were standing out of the water. When April was over the treadmill, Claudia helped her put her hands on each of the bars. She then moved April's legs to be between the bars and stood behind her. "April, can you stand by pulling yourself up to the bars?"

Sam was on her right side. "April, can you stand? Can you sense your feet on the bottom?"

April closed her eyes. "I think I can." She smiled. "I can feel my left foot. Maybe I can feel my right?"

Claudia on her left side now, stretched to push the start button. "I'm going to turn the treadmill on tortoise pace. I want you to mimic the movement you just had on the Zombie Walker."

April laughed.

The bottom half of her body moved backward with the treadmill. Both Claudia and Sam were holding her arms and had their arms around her waist. She concentrated and her left foot moved forward. Sam helped her right leg move forward. It was a strenuous few minutes before Claudia pushed the stop button.

"Wow, that felt great," April said. "Can we go some more?"

Claudia looked at Sam. April turned to look at Sam. She arched her eyebrows and smiled. "Please?"

Sam nodded. "Yes!"

April bit her lip and concentrated on her hips and feet.

After ten more minutes, Claudia pushed the stop button again.

"You did really well. The water is buoying you up. But just the same, you are getting some stimulation of your nerves and strength to your muscles. Let's get you dried off. We'll do a few more exercises, then you are free to go home," Tessa said.

***

After an additional two weeks, April was able to move her ankle and knee on her left side, but her steps remained challenging. On her right. her foot would not step naturally. She had the ability to raise her right leg from her hip, but her foot would descend toe to heel. The doctors were "cautiously optimistic" this would change. Her left side was stronger. Eric and Tessa were having her work on different machines, but her left side was doing most of the work. All the weights were light. Three times a week, she would do the Zombie Walk or go to the pool.

***

Marcie told April she needed research done on the culture of bullying and asked her to do it. The good thing was it was information she needed for her Extended Essay. April was surprised to learn how much bullying was a global issue, and that one in three kids were bullied at least once a month. She learned targets of bullying are children who are considered different by their peers. They could be kids with low self-esteem or are less popular. They could have disabilities or be LGTBQ. She found articles about bullying in India, Brazil,

Argentina, and in Asian countries. She looked up information about bullies themselves. They had risks too. They exhibited anti-social behavior and could grow up to have a tendency to have problems of holding a job, more issues concerning relationships, and are inclined to have a substance abuse disorder.

April did some research by sitting in the open area by the cafeteria called the commons and studied other kids. She pretended to be working, but she noticed for the first time kids who sat by themselves. She also saw groups of kids and how they separated themselves. Of course, understandably, kids who spoke different languages hung together. With other groups, she tried to guess what made them friends. She sat in the library, another area where kids gathered. She watched a football player she knew flick the ear of a small kid, laughing, and walking away. It reminded her out of the thirty people in the library, ten would be bullied this month. She wondered what made that football player pick on the smaller kid.

"Hi, April."

April had positioned herself where she observed most of the library's open area. She turned to see Madison. "Hi, Maddie."

Madison sat in a chair beside April. "What were you writing?"

"Oh, I'm working on my essay for class. What are you doing in here? Usually, you're in the commons."

Madison looked behind her. "I was looking for the girls, but they may have gone to the weight room. How're you doing?"

"I'm doing physical therapy, studying. How about you?"

Madison shrugged and turned again to look behind her. "I would've been able to play for the playoffs."

"Would have?"

"We didn't make them."

"Oh! I'm sorry. How's Randy?"

"We broke up."

Maddie's fingers drummed the armchair.

"You did? Oh my god. I hadn't heard that. When?"

"Right after prom. It didn't last long after…well, all the pictures and stuff."

"Geez, I'm sorry."

"Well, I gotta go."

April watched as Madison walked to the doors of the library. Something had changed. Maddie had always been so sure of herself. So together. Today, she seemed hyper. Her skin, normally healthy-looking, was blotchy. Maddie had not met her eyes once as they talked. She kept looking over April's shoulder or to the sides. She wondered how Madison had dealt with her emotions when all those pictures were circulating. She looked at her phone and realized it was time she needed to leave. Her ride would be coming to take her to physical therapy.

In the car, she texted Ashley. She wanted to ask about what else she hadn't heard about Madison.

Hey, did you need something? Ashley texted April later that night.
I saw Maddy today. What's up with her?
Her team's pissed at her.
?
They lost their last four games because she was suspended.
?
That's what they're blaming it on. Did you see other pix?
What other pix?
There were other drunken pix that went around of her hanging on other guys at the prom.
That's why R. ditched her.
Yup. Did you know her parents weren't home and couldn't pick her up?
No!
A chaperone took her home.
Yikes.
Sad.

***

Eric wanted April to use her walker. They had been continually working to strengthen her arms. Now, he was concentrating on strengthening her ankles. Using a band, he would have her push against the band with the ball of her foot. When she moved the band to her right foot, Eric stopped her. "Wait a minute. I want to try something."

He pushed the stool close to the bottom of the table where she was sitting. He massaged the bridge of her right foot. "What do you feel, April?"

At first, she shook her head. "I'm applying mild pressure to this area. Do you feel it?"

"No, not really."

"Lift the toes on your right foot, April."

"No, your foot is pointing down right now. Lift it parallel to the floor."

"I can't, Eric."

Eric ran his hand up the lower outer area of her left leg. He then did the same to the right leg. April watched him. "Tell me what you feel."

"I can feel you running your hand better on the left side than on the right side."

"Okay."

He took her shoes and socks off. He placed his fingers between the webbing of her first and second toes of her left foot.

April giggled and her foot jolted. "I'm sorry, I've always been ticklish on my left side."

Eric smiled. "Okay, let's try your right side."

"I see you're doing the same thing, but I'm not feeling anything."

"April, I want to have some tests done."

"Okay…"

"There is what is called a peroneal nerve in your legs and feet. It may not be working well, so I would like to have it assessed. We can start with a CT scan of your foot. You have two bones in your calf, the tibia and the fibula. There may be swelling near the ankle, trapping the peroneal nerve. Why I'm not sure. I'm also going to suggest a NCV. That's a nerve conduction velocity test, and an EMG test. If both are okayed, it will help us determine where along the nerve there's an injury."

"So, somehow, that nerve may not have recovered from the incident."

"Yes, running some tests will allow us to assess this."

April nodded. "It won't stop me from walking though, will it?"

Eric looked up at her. He scanned her face with his eyes. "No, April. You will walk again."

32

Ben

Ben and Terry walked down the classroom wing. Terry had intercepted Ben as he came in from the cafeteria. "Ben, come with me. I need to show you something."

Ben had little reason to come to this work area since his classes took place online, and he spent most of his day in the library. The sterile gray hall looked like any other institution, but through door windows, Ben witnessed inmates as they worked in the classrooms. Some were taking notes from a teacher. In a welding lab, men wore iron masks and used torches. "You enjoy watching them?"

Ben nodded. "It looks hot. I've never seen metal turn yellow before."

"They do many things there."

"The guys learning about auto mechanics are learning computer technology, too. Let's walk down there."

Ben followed him to the end of the hall. Terry opened the door and encouraged Ben to go in. It smelled of exhaust and grease. The open garage door allowed fresh air to combat the exhaust fumes. Several cars were parked inside with instructors and guards interspersed with inmates. There was a red Ford Explorer situated on a lift.

"My mom didn't think I should drive. She didn't think I would make good decisions."

"You've said that before."

"Yes."

"Do you think you could now?"

"I don't know."

145

Ben recognized Keno standing under one car, looking up. An instructor pointed to something. "What are they fixing there?"

Terry looked at where Ben was pointing. "Probably the muffler."

They doubled back down the hall, and Ben stopped at a window. "There's our garden," Ben said.

"Looks like you'll be harvesting soon. You guys are doing well out there."

"Professor Knight tells us we reap what we sow."

"Sounds like good advice."

Ben smiled. "There's dogs."

The training areas for inmates to work with dogs were located on the opposite side of the garden. "They teach them the basic commands. The kennels are in another area. Ben, those dogs will go to good homes. They don't stay here very long."

"That one looks like a police dog."

"Which one?"

He pointed to a shepherd mix. "Hm, maybe. Now we need for you to walk over here."

The men walked briefly, and Terry unlocked a classroom. Ben followed Terry into the room with eighteen computers in three rows. Ben stood still and stared. "What do you think?" Terry said.

"Will classes be in here?"

"Yes, can you troubleshoot these computers for us, Ben?"

"I think so."

"They're on our server. They have security on them and will be used by inmates for class. It's our first computer lab. We'll need blocks of time for inmates to use when they sign up."

"So, guards will be in here."

"Well, yes."

"I won't have to teach."

Terry laughed. "No, Ben. You won't need to teach."

They walked down to the library. It was near the hub where the building transitioned to the administration wing. Ben let Terry unlock the door. Both stood at the threshold of the room and stared. Books were scattered, creating a burst of color everywhere on the floor. Tables had been toppled, and chairs lay on their sides. The desk, where the computer was supposed to be, was even flipped over. The computer keyboard was smashed. The Dell and the monitor were on the floor. Terry gazed upwards towards the camera positioned above the bookshelves. A book had been placed in front of it. "Stay here."

Terry ran down to the guard surveillance room. He threw open the door and saw the monitor covering the library had a black-and-white image of a room with books. "For the love of God, can't you guys see that's a picture?" He said to the guards inside.

His eyes scanned the other monitors. He saw movement in most of them. He turned and left the room. The guards sat gaping at the library monitor.

Terry walked straight to the warden's office in the Administration area. He knocked on the door. "Hi, Terry. What do you need?"

Warden Teaberry had papers in front of him and a laptop by his elbow. "Come and see this," Terry said.

"You sure? I'm up to my ears here."

"No, you have to see this."

Teaberry stood and followed Terry to the guard surveillance room. Jerry Smithson, the guard supervisor, had arrived. "What's going on, Jerry?"

"These guys didn't realize the library monitor featured a picture."

"Well, you should take a look at the library."

They all turned to Terry. Terry left the room, and Jerry and Teaberry followed.

Ben had righted three tables. He stacked the books according to genre on each table. The chairs remained on their sides, and he had yet to touch the computer.

All three men stood at the door as Ben worked. "Jerry, how do you explain this happening?" The warden said.

"The noise should've caused someone to be alerted," Terry said.

Jerry was shaking his head. His eyes scanned the mess in the room. "Well, first, someone had to find that picture and be aware our monitors are black and white."

"Easy to figure that out," Teaberry said.

"The computer is on the cloud," Ben said.

"What?" Jerry said.

"Well, if it wasn't from now on, it will be," Teaberry said.

"I was thinking I could look up the books I checked out and see if there were any pictures in them."

"Ben, how did you know about the picture?" Terry said.

"He said something about a picture," Ben said, nodding toward Jerry.

Terry smirked. "We forget you don't talk much, but you listen. Help me with this."

Teaberry, Jerry, and Terry lifted the desk. "Now, let's look at this computer."

He placed the computer on the desk. The monitor remained undamaged. The computer's side had a mark, but it was in good repair. "Ben, put the cables back in order. I'll go get a keyboard from the other room. We can replace it from there."

Jerry watched as Ben worked. "They didn't smash the monitor and had to unscrew the cables, so they didn't mean to destroy the computer. But why would inmates go after the library? And when?"

"I guess we have a mystery here. The why is not as important as how," said Teaberry.

"Oh, I don't know if you need the why, but the how might lead you to the who and the when."

Terry handed Ben the keyboard he had retrieved from the other room. "Warden, if it's okay with you, I will ask Ben's cellmate, Brody Mercury, to help Ben put things back in order."

Teaberry nodded. "In the meantime, we need to figure out what guards allowed this to happen."

Brody and Ben worked on shelving books for the next three days. Ben had talked about how the library needed to be reorganized like the Springridge library, and this incident gave him a chance to do that. He had a separate area for the Dayton borrowed books, which had to be organized similarly. Ben then set about recording all the book titles on the computer and their classification. All this put him behind in his classes, so he worked to catch up until dinner while Chee and Brody kept him company. Chee read a book. Brody played solitaire.

Chee and Brody talked about having a game of cards after dinner as they walked to the cafeteria. Three other men leaving the cafeteria shifted to the three men's side of the hall. Two guys drove between Chee and Brody and threw their shoulders into them. Chee deflected the guy who pushed into him. Brody ricocheted into Ben. Both flew into the wall.

Poised to continue the fight, Chee watched as three inmates hurried away. He walked over to Brody and Ben. "Recognize them?"

Brody shook his head no. After they had gotten their food, Brody winced as he picked up his tray to go to a table. "What did you do? Chee said.

"I jammed my wrist when I hit the wall."

"Let me see," Chee said. He turned Brody's wrist over and flexed it. Again, Brody winced. It was already turning a bluish color. "It's not broken, but you have a bad sprain."

"Ben, how are you?"

"I'm okay."

Over cards that night, one player asked about Brody's wrist. He shrugged. Chee looked over his cards at Brody. "Let's not make a big deal out of it, guys. It will bring more down on us."

***

Ben was rinsing his hair under the shower the following day when he was grabbed and held in place by his chin and neck. The shower was turned to cold. Ben thrashed with his arms, trying to break the hold on him, when he heard, "I'll call anyone any name I want, bird brain."

Brody and Chee hit Keno square with their shoulders. Keno threw Ben into two other men, taking showers. Ben, blinded by water in his eyes, lost his balance and fell. He tried to stop and catch himself, but he turned and hit the back of his head. Chee and Brody lifted him to his feet. They guided him out of the shower. Chee snagged a towel and gave it to him. Ben wiped his eyes. Brody said, "Keep quiet, Ben. Don't give him the satisfaction."

"What are the chances a guard saw that?" Chee said.

"Not with all that steam."

"He told me he could call anybody any name he wants," Ben said.

Brody shook his head. "Okay, at least he didn't turn the faucet to hotter water."

They were harvesting red tomatoes when Ben stopped and rubbed his head. "My head hurts."

Brody touched the back of his head. "You've got a bump there."

"I want to go to the infirmary."

"You can't. You'd explain what happened, and we all might get in trouble."

Ben rubbed the back of his head.

***

Ben came into Terry's office the day after. As usual, he walked to the chair facing the windows. When he put his head back, he winced. Terry caught it.

"What's up?"

"Huh?"

"Did you hurt your head?

Ben was silent.

"Okay. Want to tell me what happened?"

"No."

"How's the library going?"

"Fine."

"How are classes going?"

"Fine."

Terry watched Ben for a minute. Ben looked at the floor.

"Did Brody tell you that you would get in trouble if you told?"

"Yes."

Terry nodded. He stood and walked behind Ben. He touched his head.

"Ow."

"Did someone hit you?"

"No."

"Okay, I won't ask you any more questions. Let's talk more about how your classes are going."

"They're fine."

Terry approached the credenza and picked up a thin,

elongated box. "Here's the keyboard we've been waiting for."
"It took a month."
"I know."
"Can I take it down to the classroom?"
"Well, we're not accomplishing much here today, so yes. Go."

***

"Did you manage to figure out how that happened?" Warden Teaberry called Terry and Jerry Smithson to update him on what they found about the attack on the library.
"I have observed the guards, and we've had extensive interviews with all the guards on duty during the times it might have occurred," Jerry said.
"Three of them are considered suspect," Terry said.
"What do you mean?" Teaberry asked.
"He means the three lack clear duty reports," Jerry said.
"What does that mean?"
"The guys are without detailed reports on their whereabouts that night," Terry said. "And they're not forthcoming. It's my opinion they were involved. Jerry thinks they don't write well. I would like to have them terminated."
"We can't do that!" Jerry said.
"Why not?" Terry asked.
"Because of the union. We would have to prove it's just cause," Teaberry said.
"Yes."
"So, if they sue us, at least they're out of here!" Terry said.
Teaberry stood and walked to the windows of his office. He stroked his beard for several minutes. "Not necessarily. I'm going to suspend them for incomplete reports. In the interim, I will ask for them to be transferred to another facility. I'll make sure my report of the situation has what we suspect will follow them."
"But doesn't that kick the can down the road?" Terry said.
"Yes, but maybe they'll quit," said Teaberry.
"Okay, what about the prisoners who were involved?"
"Can we go back and see who put the book in front of the camera?"

"We have that, but it's dark."
"Can we have it lightened enough to see who it is?"
Terry and Jerry nodded. Jerry said, "It looks like Bailey."
Terry shook his head. "That weak son of a gun hangs with Keno."

33

April

Getting ready for graduation was a major event, however, the gym arrangement would be different in the stadium where they would hold the ceremony. April's stomach fluttered. Mr. Trundle assured her that everything would go smoothly. "Someone will help you navigate the turf, and we have a lift on the side where you and your wheelchair would be brought up on stage."

"Have you ever had this type of situation before?"

"April, other students preferred I come down the stairs to hand them their diplomas."

"But I don't want that. I want to be up on stage like everyone else."

She had mentioned her concerns to her parents at dinner the night before. "Don't worry, April. I'll follow up with Mr. Trundle."

"No, Dad. I'll handle it."

Adele looked over her glass of water at Malaki, raising one eyebrow. Malaki smiled and nodded. "Okay, April. I'll let you handle it."

***

Today, when she and Ashley entered the gym for rehearsal, April noticed a chair was missing at the end row.

Mr. Trundle yelled over the din of students. "Everyone, get in your seats."

Faculty members were helping funnel seniors into their

rows. "I'd better go," said Ashley.

"I'll catch up with you after this."

April maneuvered her wheelchair between students as she headed for the space she saw in the back row,"No, ma'am. You are down the middle aisle where the S's are," said Mrs. Winslow. "Let me help you."

April twisted to see her IB Literature Year Two teacher smiling down at her. She nodded to her. As Mrs. Winslow positioned April's chair at the end of the S row, she reflected on how Mrs. Winslow beamed while she shared her Extended Essay titled "Bullying: A Global Issue to Be Solved Not Brushed Aside." She had invited Mrs. Reynolds to be her Community Mentor because the media could be one aspect to help solve the issue. She had requested Ashley to be a senior student assessor and Tricia, known for her mean demeanor, to be her junior assessor. Of course, April didn't know if it would make a difference in her attitude, but she hoped it would.

After practice, Mr. Trundle brought a girl to meet April. "April, we decided having you at the end of the S's wouldn't work. We need you up two more rows to get you on stage in time for your name to be called. This is Phoebe Quentin. She'll help you on the turf and to the lift. Phoebe is a junior."

"Phoebe, I've met you before. You're an IB Literature Year One."

"I heard your presentation and volunteered to help. I'll meet you in the gym before we go outside."

"Thanks, Phoebe."

As she walked away, April noticed Phoebe limp. She thought she *might have a* sports injury. As April turned her wheelchair and pushed it toward the gym door, the smell of pizza wafted into the space from the cafeteria. She realized how hungry she was.

***

The eighty-degree weather made the day of commencement perfect. Everyone looked so nice in their caps and gowns. One teacher said one hundred and twenty-two seniors were graduating today. Having graduation in the stadium posed a threat every year, and the stories of years past were filled with disappointment and humor. But only fond memories will be made this year.

Phoebe met her in the gym so she could help April to the stadium. She was dressed in a red dress, which made her blend in with the red robes of the senior girls. As they waited, April asked Phoebe why she volunteered. "April, when I was three, I was hit by a car. My right leg was crushed. Thank God, they saved it, but as I grew, it didn't grow as long as my left. It's only an inch difference, but I limp even with a lift or special shoes. My knee doesn't have all the flexibility it should have."

"Geez, Phoebe. I thought you'd say you fell or sprained your ankle."

Phoebe laughed. "On no. I loved your essay because I've had quite a few nicknames growing up. Or because I couldn't run, kids teased me."

"And now?"

"Well, just as my mom told me, it doesn't matter as much now, and the IB kids don't seem to care. I've found some good friends."

"Good. I'm glad you're helping me today."

"Me too."

The orchestra played as the seniors walked into the stadium and to their seats. Phoebe pushed April into the stadium. A slight commotion occurred when the teens found a chair missing at the end of their row. Once they realized the space was for April, the students in the row settled down, but they became concerned again, thinking Phoebe needed to be added to the row. Phoebe and April explained she would not sit there with them. As the chorus sang, the obligatory beach balls started bouncing from one person to another. They ended up stuffed under chairs as the speakers began. The Superintendent, Principal, and Class President all took their turns. The excitement filled the air when Trundle asked the first row to stand, and the first seniors made their way up the front stairs to receive their diplomas. Phoebe came to April when her row stood. She pushed April to the side where the lift waited. Eric and Tessa were waiting. They took over from Phoebe. Braking the wheelchair, Eric nodded to the person responsible to operate the lift. Tessa and Eric rose with April.

Tessa leaned over. "Nervous?"

April said, "No, excited."

"April, you'll be on stage right."
"Okay. What we planned will work."
"Yup."

April was hidden by the teachers, who were handing out diplomas. As the three students before her were called, Eric opened her walker. Eric and Tessa helped April out of her chair. April gripped the walker. Mr. Johnson, the assistant principal, did a double take when he saw April standing between Eric and Tessa. He smiled and nodded.

"April Simmons."

April stepped forward with her left foot and hesitated. Eric grasped her elbow. "It's okay, April. You can do this,"

She lifted her right foot, which fell toes first. As she placed her weight on it, she moved her walker forward. Eric held her elbow as she moved her left foot forward. Tessa moved forward. April shook her head no. Eric put his arm around her waist. "You're okay. Let's go get that diploma."

April and Eric crept across the stage. When April reached Mr. Trundle, she realized everyone in the stadium seats were on their feet, applauding. She looked out to see all her classmates standing. Mr. Trundle's eyes were full of tears. She reached out her right hand. He grasped her hand in both of his. "Congratulations, April."

"Thank you, Mr. Trundle."

Eric helped her step forward. Mr. Trundle stepped forward with them and posed with April in the standard graduating senior pose. Flashes flooded the scene. Tessa joined them at center stage, took the diploma, and walked back to April's wheelchair with April and Eric. Eric clicked the walker shut as Tessa guided April back into her chair.

As the lift descended, Tessa and Eric took turns giving April a hug. "Well done!"

Phoebe pushed April past the stage where her mom and dad waited. Her mother was in tears, and her dad's eyes were red. Ashley and Payton had left their seats to give her a hug.

Phoebe returned April to her place as the rest of the class received their diplomas. April teared up when the senior class president led everyone in moving their tassels to signify they had graduated. She had done it.

34

Ben

Terry sat at the edge of his chair while Ben sat with two feet on the ground and both his hands on the armrests.

"Look, Ben. We know you've been pushed around and harassed by Keno and his buddies. Why don't you say something?"

His question was met with Ben's stony silence.

"The warden can't put them in solitary unless you say something."

"No."

"Why not?"

"Brody and Chee say not to."

Terry sighed. "They assume it will escalate."

Ben was looking to the side. "Ben, can you look at me?"

He turned his head and complied. As fast as he met Terry's gaze, he looked down.

"Okay. The warden and I are afraid if things get worse, Brody, or you will get hurt."

Ben didn't respond.

"Okay, never mind. You've both already been hurt. How about you both could get hurt worse? The only reason Chee hasn't been hurt is because they can't catch him unaware."

"We have to do better."

"You two are not as good as Chee is. This isn't a Bruce Lee movie, for God's sake!"

"The guys keep moving the keys on the keyboards around."

"What?"

"The guys keep moving the keys…"

"I heard you. Is that all you have to say?"

"I added thirty more books to the catalog."

Terry nodded. "Good. Mrs. Yarnell is doing a good job sending books that are not being used a lot in Springridge. The warden appreciates her efforts."

"She's asked for donations from the community. She says she's had a sympathetic response."

"Good."

"Could we get Kindles for audiobooks? She said that would also be good to have."

Terry sat back in his chair and placed his hand on his forehead between his eyes.

"Ben, we are talking about your safety."

"Brody and Chee say not to say anything."

Terry looked up. "Maybe I should talk to them."

***

The guards talked as they observed the inmates working, pulling up carrots and onions. Brody and Ben were assigned to pull out the tomato plants that were no longer bearing fruit. They were to turn the soil over and make sure the clumps were chopped up.

All the tomato plants were in a pile, ready to be composted. Brody was turning the soil over. As he left one line of the garden, Ben started chopping the piles. Soon, Brody and Ben were at opposite ends of the thirty-foot garden. Three of the men who were assigned to the carrots and onions walked over to Ben.

"Ben, can we borrow your hoe?"

Ben kept chopping. "No, the guards told us not to give our tools to anyone else."

"Come on, man. We need to loosen the soil to get some carrots and onions out."

Ben ignored them and kept working.

The men walked away.

"Hey, Brain."

Ben kept chopping. Keno looked to the left and then the right. "I said, Brain."

Ben ignored him. Keno reached down and grabbed the hoe. Ben paused and then turned and looked up at Keno. "The guard said not to let anyone have the tools but us."

He reached for it, but Keno lifted it to the opposite side.

"My guys need the hoe."

Ben walked in front of Keno and extended himself to reach for the hoe again. "No, the guard said…"

"I don't care what the guard said, Brain."

Ben side-stepped to the side where Keno had placed the hoe. "No, the guard said…"

Keno swung and hit Ben in the mouth with the end of the hoe handle. "And I said, my guys need it."

Ben's bottom lip split. Blood trickled down his chin. Keno lifted the hoe and placed both hands on its handle. He swung the hoe at Ben's head. Ben ducked. He stayed low and butted Keno in the stomach with his head. Keno took a step back. Keno's face registered surprise, but then he advanced on Ben. The guards, frozen in place at first, came alive and yelled. "Hey!"

They ran toward the two as Keno punched Ben. His punch raised Ben up and knocked him to the ground. Keno fell on Ben. He placed the hoe handle across Ben's neck. Ben kicked both legs and had his hands on either side of the handle, trying to release the pressure on his neck.

Brody looked up at the guards' yell. He saw Ben fall and struggle against Keno's stranglehold. Racing up to the two men on the ground, Brody beat the guards and swung his shovel to hit Keno's shoulder. As the shovel arched, Keno saw Brody's shadow and looked up. The back of the shovel hit Keno full in the face. Keno's nose and jaw shattered at the blow.

The guards were on Brody in seconds. Keno fell to the side, blood spurting and covering Ben and the hoe handle. Ben lifted the hoe handle off his neck and lay unmoving. Brody didn't fight the guards. He stared at the sight of Keno's crushed face. He was as still as Ben, his hands hanging at his side. The shovel at his feet.

A guard kneeled to check on Ben. He placed his hand on

Ben's neck to check Ben's pulse. Ben pushed his hand away. "This guy's mouth is bleeding but seems okay."

He went to Keno and checked his pulse at the wrist. "Call 911. I can't find his pulse. I'm not going to touch his neck."

"Are you going to give him CPR?"

"Yeah, right? What if his heart hasn't stopped?"

Two men in white burst through the prison doors to the outside. Other guards were also running toward the men. The guard with Brody yelled into his radio, "We need an ambulance!"

On administering to the men, one nurse yelled, "This inmate needs a tracheostomy. I can't find his pulse."

The other nurse was tending to Ben. "This one has a split lip and a couple of loose teeth."

Terry and Warden Teaberry had reacted to the alarm call and were seen jogging to the garden area. An ambulance passed them, jumping the curb. One EMT was quick to create an air passage for Keno. His partner had an AED ready. The sound of a shirt ripping. More yelling. "Clear!" Counting. "Clear!" The EMT bent over Keno, looked at Teaberry, and said, "He's gone."

Teaberry told the EMTs to tend to Ben and then take him to the hospital to be examined. "I'll send a guard with you. In the meantime, I'll wait for the coroner."

The EMT closest to Ben tried to take his arm. Ben pulled away. Terry said, "Ben, they're going to fix you up." He turned to Teaberry. "I'll go with him. Send a guard along as soon as you can. He'll be okay."

Teaberry shook his head. "It's protocol." He said to the guard, "You go with Franklin." To another, he said, "Take Brody to his cell. Post a guard. I'm not sure who we're protecting here."

Brody's face was ashen, his eyes blank. He stood tottering with his arms hanging at his sides. Teaberry looked at Brody. "Better yet, take him to the infirmary. He's about to keel over in shock but stay with him."

35

April

With high school over, April had to decide what she would do next. She was determined to continue to college. No way would her present situation stop her from going on to her future. She talked to Eric and Tessa about studying physical therapy but decided that was not what she wanted to do. Being around the news station with Marcie and Greg was exciting, but research was what she liked. The problem of bullying intrigued her. But she didn't see how that could be a primary field of study. Counseling was a possibility. Would she able to perform tasks similar to her dad's research? He researched treatments for Alzheimer's and Aphasia. Did it require her to earn a medical degree? There was still so much she didn't know.

After all the tests Eric suggested had been run, it was determined the perineal nerve was an issue. Even with physical therapy, the nerve was not responding.

"What can we do about it? Does this mean I can't drive?"

April felt anxious. She had come so far. Is there a chance for this to be permanent? Seated in Eric's office with Tessa and her parents, April leaned forward as she tried to process what Eric had told her.

"April, you have made impressive progress, and there are ways we can still help you. They make a brace that will stop your foot from dropping, making it easier for you to walk. As far as driving is concerned, there are hand-controlled vehicles. Any type of car can be adapted. You'll need a qualified person

161

to assess your needs."

April looked at her dad, who moved up to the edge of his chair. "Honey, we will do this when you're ready. Your mom and I want you to be independent."

"Are you going to stay here for college?" Eric asked.

April said, "Yes. At least for my bachelor's degree."

"Good! Then we will continue strengthening your legs and concentrating on your balance. One of the biggest dangers of having a drop foot is tripping."

"I'll always have to use a cane, though."

"Probably."

"Well, then," April sat up straight and smiled at everyone, "I'll just buy the sharpest, brightest color, sexiest cane there is."

They returned her smile. "Any idea of what you are going to major in?"

Malaki said, "I've advised her to talk to a counselor at MSU so that she can define a direction. For starters, she'll get her Gen. Eds., but the good news is that she'll be a sophomore second semester because of her advanced classes in high school."

"I'm researching social psychology."

"Wow. That's super, April." Eric stood. "We'll work out a schedule for you to come in. Make sure you still do your exercises at home. What will you do this summer?"

"I'm going to take an online class and hope to hang out with some friends."

"Wouldn't be friends we saw at graduation?"

April nodded and said, "Oh, yes."

Malaki shook hands with Eric and Tessa. "Thank you. We'll contact you to set up that schedule."

He reached down to steady April's walker as she pushed herself up from the chair. "Thank you, guys."

36

Ben

Ben returned to prison the next day. Terry met the van. Ben had two black eyes, swollen lips with a bluish tint, and a horizontal stripe of deep purple around his neck.

"The doctor said you were lucky Keno didn't crush your windpipe. I guess working out with Chee and Brody helped you."

Ben said nothing. They walked to the infirmary to check and make sure the prescriptions the hospital ordered were on file. The doctor had read the file sent from the hospital and took a quick once-over of Ben. "Ben, you'll come here twice a day for your meds. One is for pain. Where would you say your pain is right now?"

Ben didn't answer. "Ben, on a scale from 1 to 10, 10 being terrible, what would you say your pain is?" Terry asked.

Trying not to move his mouth, Ben said, "Seven."

"Around your mouth?"

Ben nodded. "Okay, you take soft food for lunch and dinner," Terry said.

They walked to Ben's cell. "Ben, Brody won't be there today."

"What's going to happen to him?"

"Brody was a nonviolent offender when he came here. He racked up some crimes like carjacking and was the getaway driver for a bank robbery. What sent Brody here is he stole money that he was supposed to deliver to a bank. We hope we can prove Brody first didn't mean to kill Keno, and second, he hit Keno to save you. That's why we asked for so many pictures of you at the hospital."

"Will he come back here?"

"We're not sure. Okay, why don't you rest and then get some lunch?"

"I'm going to go down to the library this afternoon."

Terry nodded. "Okay, if you're up to it."

Ben nodded. He walked to his cell and laid down on his bunk.

After resting, Ben walked to the cafeteria. As Terry suggested, he went through the line and looked at the options. Brody always encouraged Ben to eat salad, pork, green beans, or tomatoes. But Brody wasn't there. Ben chose food of smooth texture. The corn, sweet potato fries, and lima beans were gross to him. All Ben took was chicken soup. He walked with his tray to the open space of the cafeteria. Brody would encourage him to sit with different people. But Brody wasn't there. He didn't see Chee. An empty table was available, so he sat there. He became upset with himself when he realized he hadn't stopped for crackers, water, or a napkin. The first spoonful hurt his lip. He waited for it to cool. The second spoonful of soup tasted too salty. In his distress, he dripped a bit of soup on the table and didn't have a napkin to clean it. When he looked around and saw the other men eating and talking, he stood and took his tray to the deposit area. As he left, a guard asked where he was going. "I'm going to the library," he said.

The guard looked at his number. Using his radio, he checked for authorization, and nodded to Ben to go ahead.

Ben walked through the halls, stopping by checkpoints as he should. Arriving at the library, he waited for the guard from the last checkpoint to open the door. Inside, Ben stopped. His hands shook. His breath came fast and shallow. He sat at the computer and powered it up. Standing, he went to the cart that carried the approved books. Deciding to separate the nonfiction from the fiction, he pushed the cart to the first table. He ran his fingers along the colorful spines of the novels to search for an author whose name started with A. Mrs. Yarnell had taught him to do this years ago. His back was turned to the door when he heard, "Can I check out a book?"

Ben whirled around. A young black inmate with a goatee was just inside the door with a guard shadowing him. Ben nodded yes.

The inmate came and started looking at the books on the cart. "You can't check those out yet. I haven't entered them." Ben mumbled, continuing to work on the cart.

"Okay. Do you have any Sci-Fi?"

Pointing to the back of the room, Ben said, "Yes, over there."

The inmate kept turning to watch Ben and the guard as he wandered by the shelves.

"You don't have a guard following you?"

Ben didn't answer him. "Hey, why don't you have a guard following you?" He said louder.

Ben didn't answer him.

After taking a book, the prisoner walked over to Ben, who had moved to his computer.

"I need your number," Ben said.

After typing in the inmate's number, Ben took the book and keyed in the serial number of the book.

"Don't you talk to people like me?"

Ben side-eyed him. "I don't know what you mean."

The man leaned over to place his head between Ben's face and the computer. The guard moved to pull him back. Ben dropped back in his chair and crossed his wrists and hands in front of his face. "No!"

The guard pulled the young inmate in the door's direction. "Come on, you got your book. Let's go."

After ten minutes, Ben put his hands down and stared at the computer. He looked up at the camera that surveilled the room. He stood and paced the room. Seated back at the desk, he unscrewed the cable behind the computer. He followed the cable to its outlet on the monitor. Stretching it for length, he looped the end as if to store it; instead, he tied a knot. Ben walked around the library, looking above the bookshelves. He noticed the arm on the monitor, but it was thin and wouldn't hold much more than the weight of the flat screen. Then Ben saw a corner of a bookshelf that was detached a bit. He reached to catch the thick monitor plug in the gap. Tugging to ensure the plug was secure, he pulled on the knot to check if it would slide, then placed the loop around his neck. He sagged to his knees.

Ben didn't fight as his breath struggled to come into his

body. Ben blacked out.

The guard on duty was eating a donut at the guard monitoring station. His eyes wandered to each surveilled area. Something caught his eye in the library. Standing, he looked closer to concentrate on the screen's bottom left corner. Something odd was there and then gone. A rounded item with something on top came into view again. It looked like the top of a head with hair standing on end. Then it disappeared again. Maybe someone was looking for a book, he thought. But it bothered him enough to stay fixed on the shot. He realized either the person looking for a book was swaying to and fro, or something was wrong. He pressed the alarm button.

Terry was immersed in reports when the alarm sounded. On his radio, he heard, "All available guards report to the library." He emerged out of his concentration, realizing what the guard said. He scrambled out of the chair and through his office door. Running down the hall and sliding into the library, he took in the scene of two guards, one giving Ben mouth-to-mouth and another powering up an AED.

"What the hell, Ben?" He said to no one in particular.

"He's breathing!" Yelled a guard.

Terry moved out of the doorway as the medical personnel brought in a gurney and medical apparatus. The doctor wrapped a blood pressure sleeve around Ben's arm and took his vitals. The doctor looked at Terry and said, "He's back."

"Take him to the infirmary but put him on suicide watch. I'll be in to see him when you have him stable."

The doctor nodded to the medical personnel and followed the gurney out of the room.

***

Terry was sitting in Ben's chair in front of the library desk monitor. "The guards said you were still in here." Warden Teaberry said.

Terry turned to see him standing in the doorway. "I never anticipated he would do this. Damn."

"I talked to Greg Parker. He's the guard that was in here with a new inmate today. He said Blanket got in his face before he could pull him away. I looked at the tape. Ben had a defensive reaction. You'll have to see it."

"What was the time stamp?"

"Right before Ben tried to hang himself. Terry, what do you want to do?"

"I'm going to wait a bit, and then I'm going to talk to Ben."

"Terry, I don't want a suicide on my watch. Are you too invested in this guy?"

"I'd like him to survive and walk out of here someday."

***

Terry received a call from the doctor the next day. He told Terry he had Ben on some anxiety meds and suggested he visit him. Terry finished up some reports that needed to be completed and walked over to the infirmary.

Nodding to the guard, he walked to a chair and moved it over to Ben's bedside. Ben watched him place the chair and then looked away. "What the hell? Want to explain what you were thinking?"

Ben shook his head no.

"Well, you're going to have to. Brody is in trouble because he cared enough about you to protect you, and you repay him by doing this."

Ben turned his head to glare at Terry. "Oh, you didn't think of that?"

"No."

"Didn't think so. Want to tell me what made you do this?"

Ben shrugged. "Oh no. I'm not letting you off that easy. You keep saying you are a highly functioning person. Time to think it through."

"I…I just didn't want to fight anymore."

"Is that what you call fighting? Backing away? Running away?"

"I lost my house."

"Old news. Ben, we all have to fight every day. Whether it's bullies, bad habits, feeling down, or unpleasant situations. Most days are a challenge for everyone. It's the decision to keep going that gives us purpose. People here have made wrong

decisions to solve those challenges."
"Like I did. That's why I lost my house."
"And a girl needs to learn to walk again."
"You know about the girl?"
"Of course I do, Ben. And it's time we talk about her."
"Will the warden still let me run the library?"
"We'll talk to him as soon as the doctor releases you."

37

Ben

It took two weeks for Terry to release Ben from the suicide watch. Once they found out Brody had a lawyer working to get the manslaughter charges withdrawn, Terry told Ben Brody needed him to be okay, in case Ben had to testify on Brody's behalf. Ben asked to return to his cell.

Terry was working with another inmate when his cell rang. "This is Barry, the guard by cell block A. Ben Franklin has requested to see you."

"Walk him down in a half hour," Terry said.

When Ben arrived, he handed Terry a note from Mrs. Yarnell. She wrote her attorney had watched a documentary that WCMS aired. He wanted to investigate Ben's case and see if a retrial or a request for early parole was possible.

"Ben, this is great."

Ben was sitting in his usual chair, his right knee pumping. He shook his head. "Where would I go if I were released?"

"Ben, why don't we cross that bridge when we come to it?"

"Mrs. Yarnell retired from Springridge Library, so there's no guarantee I'll have a job."

"Ben, you've worked well with the Dayton system. There may be a position there.

"Then you think I should let the attorney look into my case."

"I would meet with him."

"Okay."

"Remember in the infirmary? I said we need to talk about the girl you shot?"

"She and her friends were trespassing."

Terry pressed his lips together, looked down then lifted his head, and took a deep breath. "Ben, that's true. But shooting an innocent girl?"

"I didn't shoot at her."

"No, you're right. It was an awful accident."

"I was shooting the bushes!"

"Right. Did you see the girls had left your property when you shot your gun?"

Ben stared at Terry.

"Did you? From what I hear, the girls had left and were on the sidewalk behind those bushes."

There was no movement from Ben.

"Come to grips that you were to blame, Ben."

Ben looked away, avoiding Terry's gaze.

"Let that sink in." Terry rose out of his chair and walked to his bookshelf. "I found a book for you. It's going to be our workbook." He handed the book to Ben. "Read Part 1 before our next session this Friday."

"It's Tuesday."

"Read it."

***

On Friday, Ben left the library for his one o'clock appointment with Terry. He had the book Terry had assigned him as he knocked on Terry's office door. "Open."

Terry was standing, looking out of a window, when Ben entered. "Nasty weather out there."

The rain covered his windows, and the looming clouds gave the impression it would not stop anytime soon. Ben walked over to his chair and sat. Terry turned. "Did you read the first chapters?"

Ben shrugged. "Ben, what is autism?"

"It's a bio-neurological developmental disability. It's a social and communicative disorder. I've read about it."

"But what does that mean for you, exactly?"

"I have trouble with talking and taking cues from people."

"So, what did you get out of the book?"

"High school is hard on people with ASD."

"Is that when things got hard for you?"

Ben shifted. "Kids didn't like me and stole my stuff in middle school. It got worse after my mom walked me to school."

"How did you do in school?"

"I earned A's."

"But you didn't hang with the smart kids?"

Ben shook his head. "I worked in the library when I wasn't in class."

Terry walked over to the chair facing Ben. "We're going to try something. Have you ever talked to the ladies at the grocery store? You know the cashier. Or the person you bought coffee from?"

"I don't drink coffee."

"Okay, let's talk about the person at the pharmacy."

"Why?"

"We're going to practice talking to a stranger."

"Like in the book." Ben gestured to the book on his lap.

"Yeah. Just like in the book. What did it say about small talk?"

"It's level one of communication."

"Good. Okay, what do you do when you go to the pharmacy?"

"Tell the clerk my name and birthdate."

"Let's try to practice like they did in the book. How about saying Good Morning? Or Hello?"

"Okay. Good morning."

"Good morning. How are you today? May I have your name and birthdate?"

"Benjamin Franklin. Three-seventeen-nineteen-ninety-two."

"Good Ben. According to the book, how could the clerk react?"

"She could get my medicine."

"True. Could you say fine, before you give your name and birthday?"

Ben tilted his head. "Not if I'm there for medicine."

"Okay. Um. The book gave you three responses. Do you remember them?"

"Yes, there were three responses. The clerk could return my Good Morning with a positive, neutral, or negative response."

"What would those mean in the way of gestures or facial reactions?

Ben considered Terry's question for a minute. "Positive would be if the person smiled and said Good Morning back. Neutral would be that he or she would just go get my medicine. I don't believe the person would be negative because they could lose their job."

Terry smiled. "True. I would suggest that if a person here at the prison reacts negatively, the person might not want to talk or be around anyone. Right? But it wouldn't have anything to do with you."

"It might be better to leave that person alone."

Terry nodded. "Yes. Did you read the part about how to deal with a bully?"

"Yes."

"What's your reaction?"

"I can't feel sorry for Keno. I'm sorry Brody killed him, but I don't feel sorry for him."

"You've had experiences before with bullies."

Ben moved and shifted again in his chair. "Ben, it's essential to learn to deal with people who want you to be miserable because they are. Here at Madison, it's different from the outside. Keno wanted to hurt people and got others to do the same. Brody and Chee were teaching you how to cope and defend yourself. Be aware of your surroundings and it will be like that to a point on the outside, too."

Ben was quiet. He put his hands on top of the book. "Terry, I didn't hurt anyone in Springridge, but they kept coming after me and my mother. Were they bullies?"

Terry folded his arms and stared past Ben. In a moment, his eyes came back to look at him. "You'll have to give me time to think about an answer for that, Ben. I can't guess what made kids harass you. It seems there was a bigger issue there than what's normal."

***

Sam Donahue, Esq., had been Barb Yarnell's attorney for ten years. He used to focus on family law, but his firm encouraged him to accept criminal cases five years ago. Mrs.

172

Yarnell asked him to watch the WCMS documentary because she still felt certain Ben didn't receive a fair trial. Marcie Reynold was an acquaintance, and he reached out to Marcie after the documentary aired. They determined that going through Mrs. Yarnell may help communicate with Ben. Her recommendation and encouragement would help Ben trust Sam.

Sam drove down to Madison prison on a bright fall day. He always shivered when the gates closed behind him, and he heard locks engage. As Sam watched Ben walked toward him in the meeting room, Sam noted how different Ben looked from the tape of his trial. He stood up straight and walked without hesitation. His face didn't have the cowering expression. In file tapes, Ben never looked at the judge. Today, before Ben sat down, he offered his hand to shake and looked at Sam as he shook his hand.

As they sat across from each other, Sam asked, "How are you doing in here, Ben?

"I'm okay."

"Can you tell me a little about yourself? Catch me up on your time in here."

"I work in the library. My job is to recommend books to be okayed by the warden. Once he okays them, I file them and check them in and out. I work in the garden in spring and summer when it's nice outside, but I don't know if I will next year."

Ben half closed his eyes, looking down at his hands in his lap. He tightened his mouth as he said this.

"Mrs. Yarnell said you are talking to the psychiatrist here."

"He's a counselor. Yes, I meet with Terry once or twice a week. We talk about books I've been reading."

"Oh, like what?"

"Books on how to adapt in society when you're autistic."

"Are they helping you?"

Ben nodded.

"Will you tell me about what happened that Halloween night?"

Ben brought his hands up to the table and clasped them. "Terry says that losing my house is old news."

"Okay, but Ben, I want to hear from you what happened."

"I left the lights off in the house because I didn't want any trick-or-treaters. But older kids came anyway."

"Is that the only time older kids came to your house?"

"No. The kids came all year round, but it's always worse on Halloween."

"What happened that year?"

"They soaped my windows, threw cow manure at my house and on my porch. It stunk up everything. No eggs that year, though."

"I imagine that was hard to clean."

Ben nodded. "Yes, it was." For a moment, he said nothing. "I tried chasing them away once. They ran away laughing and came back another time."

"How long did this go on?"

"Before my mom died."

"How long has that been?"

Ben sat back in his chair. Ben's hands remained on the table. Looking at his hands, he said, "Eight years."

"Ben, why didn't you call the police?"

"My mom did, but they did nothing. They would drive by a few times. But when the kids came, and she called, by the time they got there, the kids were gone. They said they would write a report." He shrugged with one shoulder. "But that's it. The kids would come back."

"I read some reports that the neighbors complained about your house's appearance. They said it helped attract the kids."

"I thought that if the outside looked scary, it would keep them away. I tried locks on the gate, but they brought lock cutters or hopped over it."

"The police report said the gate was open that Halloween night."

"Two days before, one screw on the latch broke. I didn't get to the hardware store to replace it. I was working."

"None of this was said at your trial, was it?"

"No."

"Why did you buy the rifle?

"It was my dad's. I just bought the bullets."

"What did he use it for?"

"My mom said he liked to hunt rabbits and squirrels back in the day."

"You didn't know your dad?"

"No, he left when I was five. Mom said I was behind in a lot of ways as a baby, but I wasn't diagnosed with autism until I was three. Mom thought he would send for us when he took a job in California, but all he sent was money."

"Did you ever make contact with him?"

"He sent money through a bank account. I never knew how to contact him. Once the house was paid for, the money stopped. I was twenty-one. I supported my mom until she died."

"And you never looked for him."

"I never felt I wanted to find him."

"Ben, I'm going to see what I can do." Sam stood and held out his hand to Ben. "I'll be in touch."

Ben stood and shook his hand, making sure he looked into Sam's eyes.

***

Three months later, Sam Donahue returned to visit Ben. "I've been looking into your case. I've requested what's called a Judicial Request Hearing. Please file a judicial release motion, naming me as your attorney." Sam handed him an envelope containing a sheet of instructions, paperwork, and an addressed envelope. It will take a while, and we need to ask for a few things from your friends here at the prison."

"Like what?"

"Before I get into that, I just want to stress we can only do this once. There's no second chance."

"How long will it take?"

"Judges are busy, so I'm not sure. Maybe as long as six to nine months. It could be a year."

Sam could feel Ben's knee bouncing. "Ben, these things take time."

Ben fingered the envelope. "Okay, but I'm not sure where I'll go."

"Ben, this isn't a home. It's a prison. If you can get out, you should."

Ben nods. "That's what Terry says."

"Okay, let's talk about your prison record. Are there any

infractions I should know about?"

"No, Brody and I just got into trouble once."

"Want to tell me about it?"

"Brody came back."

"Okay, good. But what happened?"

"Brody hit a guy with a shovel, and he died."

"Wow."

"Keno was choking me with a hoe."

Sam leaned forward. "Alright. Is there anything else?"

Ben bit his lower lip. He concentrated. A moment passed. And another. "No, I don't think so."

"Barb, Mrs. Yarnell mentioned she thought you may have completed a course while you were here," Sam said.

"Yes, I completed a Librarian and Information Science degree from Kent State University. It was all online."

"I guess it would have to be," Sam said. He smiled.

"I think I get what you mean," Ben said. He smiled back.

"You know, since you were in prison," Sam said.

"Oh, yes," Ben said. He nodded and swayed a bit in his chair.

Sam shifted some papers around. "I know Mrs. Yarnell will be glad to write you a recommendation. Who else should I include in my list?"

Ben was quiet again for a minute or two. "Could I ask the warden and Terry?"

"Those would be good."

"And Rick Fleming."

Sam was writing the names. "Who is Rick Fleming?"

"He was my mentor when I first came here. He left a while ago."

"Do you have an address for him?"

"I'll check with Terry."

"Okay, good. Anyone else?"

Ben shook his head.

"What will you do when you are released? It is good to have a plan."

Ben hesitated. "I don't know. I want to stay here and run the library."

"Um, Ben. That may not be possible. Why don't we table that for now."

Ben looked at the table. "No, Ben. That means we'll put that aside for now."

"Oh, okay."

"I'll get the paperwork together for you." Motioning to his legal pad, "I'll also get the recommendation requests out. Get Rick Fleming's address as soon as you can."

Ben nodded.

Sam gathered his paperwork, opened his briefcase on the table, and placed all the paperwork and notes in it. He stood. Ben stood with him and offered his hand to Sam.

Sam took it and smiled. "You're doing well, Ben."

Ben nodded and walked to the door without looking back.

38

April

A year after she graduated from Springridge High School, Killian asked April to do an interview. She wanted to let people know how April was doing. April had asked Greg and Marcie if they would interview her for the documentary, but, along with her parents, they agreed she should wait and let some time pass.

Killian: April Simmons and her friends were carrying out a senior tradition of taking selfies at the house they called the Ghost House in their town of Springridge two years ago. I have agreed to say this tradition was not sanctioned by their high school. As they were leaving the Ghost House that Halloween, she was shot by the man who lived there. The bullet paralyzed her. I believe it was time for us to check in with her.

Killian: Hi April. Catch us up on how you're doing.
April: I'm good. I'm a sophomore at The Midtown State University.
Killian: How are you doing physically?
April: I'm up and walking! (She smiles and shows her glittering scarlet and gray striped cane) I have a cane because I have a drop foot, but I'm doing well.
Killian: That's good to hear. I like your cane. For our viewers, what is drop foot?
April: My right foot drops toe to heel, putting me in danger of tripping. Around campus, I use my wheelchair because I'm slow when I'm walking. I feel more secure in my wheelchair.

Killian: Do you have a major yet?

April: Yes, I am majoring in Social Psychology.

Killian: When I talked to you before the interview, you said what happened to you sparked your interest in this area. How?

April: The documentary WCMS did about bullying and cyberbullying made me think.

Killian: You helped with the research, didn't you?

April: Yes, I read that bullying is a global issue. It's not just kids like most people assume. I mean, kids do bully. I even saw it occur while I researched, but it also happens to adults at work. Kids can learn to bully from their siblings, parents and sometimes teachers.

Killian: I remember that from the documentary. I'm amazed that the incident that paralyzed you and your research helped you think.

April: During my senior year, I would get angry. At first, I wanted to know why this happened to me. My plans for my senior year and where I was going to college were ruined. I had to concentrate on walking again, and I had to reassess a lot of things. For example, I realized I was attending college to play field hockey with my friends. I never considered what I would study.

Killian: How did you decide on Social Psychology?

April: While recovering, I worked on an essay for a class and the documentary here at WCMS. I did a lot of research on bullying and its causes. I learned that bullying is a systematic and global issue. Bullying puts kids at risk for numerous psychiatric problems, including depression, anxiety, panic disorders, suicidal thoughts or behavior, and agoraphobia. I realized that there is a correlation between bullying and kindness.

Killian: Really? What?

April: Do you remember the commercial where one person does a kindness for someone, and that person then does a kindness for another person, and it goes on. Bullying is the same. One person bullies someone, and then that person does the same, and it goes on. That's simplified, but I'd like to find out more.

Killian: That never occurred to me to think of it that way. Do you ever think about Ben Franklin, the man who shot you?

April: I'm still angry with him on some level. He caused me a lot of pain, but I'm working on dealing with that anger with a counselor. Concentrating on my schoolwork and becoming more mobile has helped a lot.

Killian: Thank you for coming today. It's so good to see you doing so well.

April: Thanks, Killian, for having me.

39

Ben

Ben, escorted by a guard, knocked on Terry's office door. "Enter."

Terry looked up to as Ben came in and walked to his usual place. "Well, it's been a while since I last saw you, about two weeks ago."

Terry put his work away in a drawer and came around his desk to sit across from Ben.

Ben was looking down at his feet. "Ben?"

"I'm supposed to ask you if you know Rick's address."

"I can get it for you. What's going on? Something wrong in the library?"

"No."

"Ben, we've worked on meeting someone's eyes when talking with them."

With this, Ben looked up. "I don't know if I want to get out."

"Okay. So, you haven't come here just to ask for Rick's address. You came to procrastinate."

Ben nodded. "Yes."

"Okay. Well, unless we can get you to acknowledge if you're remorseful about the girl you hurt, the act that put you in here, you may not get out. The judge will ask you about it."

Ben sat with his hands on the armrests of the chair. His fingers were drumming. "Can we talk about it?" Terry asked.

Ben looked off to the side and out the window. "Okay."

"Ben, three teenage girls came on your property that night."

"Yes, they were trespassing."

"Yes. The girls were not the kids who threw eggs or manure

181

at your house."

"No."

"They knocked on your door and took selfies."

"Yes, but they were trespassing."

"Yes, they were. But they did nothing but knock."

"I didn't mean to hit them."

"Yes, you were shooting at the bushes. But with those second shots, a bullet went through the bushes, and you shot a young girl."

As has happened many times before, Ben sat down and said nothing when Terry brought this up.

"Ben?"

Ben turned his face met Terry's eyes. "How is she now?"

Terry paused. "I'm not sure. I watched an interview she did on the news. She is walking again and going to The Midtown State University."

"And the others?"

"The other girls or all the other kids who bothered you?"

Ben nodded. "I have no idea. But if you leave here, you could go somewhere else other than Springridge."

Ben turned his head again to gaze out the window. Terry sat for a minute. "Ben, what if I contact Rick? Check how he's doing. I've heard he's been helping people once they're out on parole."

"That's what he wanted to do."

"I'll contact him today, and we'll go from there."

***

Ben asked the guard to lock the library. He said he would return in an hour. The guard did what Ben asked and escorted him to Terry's office. Ben knocked. "Enter."

Sitting in Ben's place was Rick. Ben smiled when he saw him.

"Wow. Terry, you mentioned to me that Ben was making progress. Can I hug you?"

"No. I'd rather you not."

"Okay, some things haven't changed."

"No."

"Ben, sit. Rick has some good news for you."

When Ben hesitates, Terry said, "Rick, why don't you sit in

this other chair."

Rick had a confused look in his eyes but got up and moved to the other chair. Ben stepped forward and sat in his usual place. "I get it," Rick said.

Terry sat behind his desk. "Ben, since we talked, I contacted Rick. He said he would gladly write you a letter, but he had another idea too. Tell him."

"Ben, I've been writing grants to help prisons and former inmates establish programs to help people acclimate back into society. One of the grants would allow you to work here as the librarian in collaboration with the Dayton Library system for a year. The money would allow you to find a place and work here."

Ben crossed his arms and patted his right arm with his left fingers. He looked off to the side at the windows. "What happens after a year?"

"We would apply to the Dayton Library system or find out if the state has enough money to support your salary. There might be another grant. Many things could happen."

"Ben, this would also go toward your success with the Judicial Release," Terry said.

"I might work here?"

Rick shifted in his seat. "Yes, Ben."

"I wouldn't go back to Springridge."

"No, you wouldn't. Ben, don't you have things in storage?"

"Yes."

"Well, you could get those things out."

"Brody has a few more years here."

"But Ben, you can't…"

"Rick, why don't we let Ben think about everything? Can you give him forty-eight hours?" Terry said.

Rick nodded. "Okay, Ben. I'll be back in forty-eight hours to answer your questions."

***

When Brody returned from his winter duty of working in the laundry area, Ben was sitting in their cell, reading. "Hey, how'd your meeting go?"

"They want to get me out."

"I know that, man. I think it's great."

"Rick was in the meeting."

"How's he doin'?

"He's fine. He might have a way for me work here and live close by."

"Whoa! You lucky son of a bitch. That's something."

"But what about…?"

"What about what?"

"You. My friends."

Brody was sitting on his bed. He looked down and smiled. "Damn. Any of us would love to have that chance, man. You know, Chee and I aren't here for life. I'm up for parole in a year. Chee has six months. By the time they decide about you, he could be out."

Ben nodded. "Come on, let's go tell Chee," Brody said.

40

Judicial Release Hearing

After gathering all the paperwork, Sam Donahue filed the petition for a Judicial Release Ben and Terry followed their usual routines since they were warned that judicial hearing was rarely granted. After six long weeks, Terry called Ben to his office.

Ben was out cleaning up the garden areas for planting. It took a while to scrape the mud from his shoes and put away tools. A guard from the garden work detail escorted Ben to Terry's office.

"Enter."

Terry motioned for the guard to know it was okay and for Ben to sit down. Terry finished the notes on his laptop and slid it into the middle drawer of his desk. "I just received a call from Sam Donahue, and they have granted you a hearing."

Ben blinked but said nothing. His knee started bouncing.

"Ben, did you hear me?"

"What now?"

Terry took a deep breath. "Ben, the hearing is set for the 26th of June. I'll notify everyone involved in this effort and hope they will be at the hearing for you. Transportation will be arranged for you. Don't get your hopes up or be concerned about this. It is rare when a release is granted. Judge Radcliffe will be the judge again. He is strict in his rulings."

"Ben, can you give me an idea of how you're feeling?"

Minutes passed before Ben said, "I'm not sure."

"That's fair."

Terry gave Ben a few more minutes to process the

information.

"I'll alert Rick. He needs to know so that the grant he discussed with you could be available for your release."

Ben's knee stopped bouncing, and he only moved his hand to rub his bottom lip. "Rick said he would help me, didn't he?"

Terry nodded. His eyes scanned Ben's face. "Ben, Rick said he would help you find temporary housing and give you rides when you need them. I'll help until you get settled and figure all this out. But you can't worry about all that. We don't know if this will happen."

***

On June 26, Terry, Warden Teaberry, Rick Fleming, Barb Yarnell, and Susie Waxman sat behind the table where Sam and Ben would sit. Sam came in and said hello to everyone and shook hands. Barb Yarnell asked him if he thought Ben would be released.

Sam held her hand in both of his. "Barb, I don't know. We have done everything we can to help him. He'll answer some questions today, and the judge will decide based on Ben's answers, as well as the information we provided him."

A door opened to an inner room. Ben was led in by a guard. He wore a nice button-down blue shirt and khaki pants. Ben looked around the white room with the black table and chairs where he and Sam would sit. He then focused on the people who were there to support him. He smiled and nodded to them. Barb Yarnell and Susie Waxman looked at each other and whispered.

When the guard led him over to where Sam stood, Ben extended his hand to Sam who took it and grasped it confidently. They both turned, pulled out their chairs, and sat facing the judge's table and chair in front of them. Sam busied himself with pulling folders from his briefcase. Ben sat with his hands out of sight.

The judge came in from another door, and everyone rose. The judge motioned for everyone to be seated. "We are here today to determine if Benjamin Franklin should receive a judicial release. Mr. Donahue, you wrote a compelling motion for Mr. Franklin. Mr. Franklin, I have some questions for you."

Ben said, "Yes, sir."

"You shot a gun out of your bedroom window on a

Halloween night two years ago. A teenage girl was hurt. How do you explain yourself?"

"I didn't mean for anyone to get hurt. I wanted to scare the girl and her friends away," Ben said.

"Do you intend to return to Springridge, where the incident occurred?"

"No, sir. I am going to stay close to Dayton."

"Doing what?"

"I am going to work for the Dayton City Library and Madison Prison, running a library and doing IT."

The judge nodded. "You had no previous infractions before this incident?"

"No, sir."

"How much did you pay the victim in restitution?"

"I sold my house and paid them $75,000."

Again, the judge nodded. "That's a lot of money." He studied Ben for a bit.

"Mr. Franklin, this motion says you are autistic. What does that mean to you?"

"It means I have trouble communicating with people and reading their expressions. I am smart, and I'm highly functional."

The judge sat back in his chair. He rested his elbows on the armrests and folded his hands over his stomach. "Mr. Franklin, do you feel remorse for shooting at those girls?"

Ben rocked in his chair and drew his hands up to the table. He folded them. First, he looked at his hands and then at the judge. "I'm sorry that I shot the one girl who I guess has struggled because of me. The shots were to scare them away. I was tired of people knocking on my doors and windows, throwing eggs at my house."

"But I understand your house was an eyesore, and it encouraged kids to bother you."

Terry shifted in his seat. Rick looked at him.

"My house wasn't always like that. I let the bushes and grass grow to keep kids away, but nothing helped."

"Why didn't you call the police?"

"I lived there with my mother until she died. She called them all the time. But the kids kept coming. The police didn't stop them."

"You aren't returning to Springridge."

"No. My friends are helping me work and stay near them."

Terry looked at Rick, nodding and smiling.

"Okay, thank you, Mr. Donahue, for submitting this motion. I will rule in a few weeks."

The judge stood and walked out of the room.

The Madison Correctional guard walked to their table and stood. "I guess we'll know in a few weeks, Ben. I think you gave the judge a lot to think about."

Ben nodded and turned to the people behind him. "Thank you for coming."

He turned to the guard, and they walked out of the room.

Rick rubbed his mouth. "Terry, what do you think?"

Terry shrugged. "I was nervous when the judge questioned him with some triggers, but I think Ben handled himself well. Honestly, he surprised me."

Springridge Gazette

Springridge Gazette

Detective Suspended for Domestic Abuse
By Robert Cunningham

A Springridge detective was suspended pending the investigation of domestic violence. Lynette Bennet called 911 Saturday night after her husband, Detective Darnell Bennet, allegedly beat her and then locked her in the basement.

Police responded to the emergency call of a domestic disturbance. Mrs. Bennet was rushed to Mercy Hospital with lacerations of the face and possible internal bleeding. Bennet was at the scene with a blood alcohol level of .16.

Former Owner of the *Ghost House* Paroled
By Robert Cunningham

Benjamin Franklin, former owner of 1209 Brueberry Lane, has been released early from Madison Correctional Facility.

Franklin had served for two years.

Franklin was convicted of three counts of felonious assault. Three girls were trying to complete a senior prank when Franklin shot and wounded April Simmons, then 18. His original sentence was for fifteen years. Franklin's judicial release was granted uncontested.

Thank you

Thank you for buying this book. If you liked it, please leave a review on Amazon or Barnes and Nobles.

To receive special offers, bonus content, and information about new releases and other great reads, sign up for her Hello There! Substack at sandrakhorn@substack.com or going to her website at SandraKHorn.net.

Acknowledgements

Acknowledgements

I have read many times that writing a book is a lonely job. In my case, I have a lot of help. My neighbor, David Janning, was an EMT. I walked up to him one day, and after telling him I was writing another book, I asked him how he would treat a victim who was shot. He is now studying to be a nurse. He will be amazing. Another acquaintance is Eric Hrenko, a physical therapist, who helped me establish April's injuries. Thank you to Maureen Severns and Dawn Petril for assisting me and encouraging me to write a story including a man with neurodiversity. Thank you to Nathaniel Petril for being special and telling me about your dreams of going to DisneyWorld.

Thank you to my beta readers, Carol Oswald and Mara Holt. They are both sticklers with plot lines, words, and punctuation, and their support is invaluable. Every month, the Women's Connection Writer's Group listened to my paragraphs and chapters, giving me ideas and positive reactions. Thank you to Susie Collins, Donna Kayne, Roberta Kayne, Mary Greenlee, Sharon Mast, and Mara Holt.

Thank you to my friends in the Ohio Branch of the National League of American Pen Women: Dawn Petri, Darlene Yeager-Torre, Bev Goldie, Gayle Holton, and Karin Dahl. These ladies have so much creative energy that it spills over into my writing.

And to my husband C. Edward. I would disappear for hours to write or research. Thank you for your constant loving support.

The challenge of writing this type of story is feeling that the information has to be correct. The following are the websites and books I read and let guide me as I wrote. Any errors are mine.

Centers for Disease Control and Prevention, Suicide Prevention, "Youth Suicide" [online]

Dickinson, Matt, The Independent, "Research finds bullying link to child suicides" [online]

Donaldson James, Susan ABC News, Health, "Teen Commits Suicide Due to Bullying:
   Parents Sue School for Son's Death" [online]

Eckholm, Eric and Katie Zezima, The New York Times, "6 Teenagers Are Charged After Classmate's Suicide" [online]

Hunt, Jaclyn. *Life Coaching for Adults on the Autism Spectrum: Discovering Your True Potential.ASD* Life Coaches LLC (December 5, 2021)

Inbar Michael, MSNBC Today, "Sexting bullying cited in teen's suicide" [online]

Nemours, KidsHealth, "Helping Kids Deal with Bullies" [online]

Price, Devon. *Unmasking Autism: Discovering the New Faces of Neurodiversity. Harmony (April 5, 2022)*

Prinzant, Barry, Ph.D, and Tom Fields-Meyer. *Uniquely Human* A Different Way of Seeing Autism Simon & Schuster; 1st edition (August 4, 2015)

Steele, Geoffrey. *The Unstoppable Eddie Fugate.* Geoffrey Steele (June 20, 2023)

"Understanding Bullying, https://jedfoundation.org/resource/understanding-bullying/?gad_source=1&gclid=Cj0KCQiAy9msBhD0ARIsA Nbk0A-dQ2XE0X_ofW_cpr_LgMCyAq5TVomHKis_q9MDjSJ2i7b0zn UfcqQaAgzHEALw_wcB

WebMD, Depression Guide, "Recognizing the Warning Signs of Suicide" [online]
    Yale University, Office of Public Affairs, "Bullying-Suicide Link Explored in New Study by Researchers at Yale" [online]

Also by Sandra K-Horn

Undercover : Becoming Street Smart in Central Ohio
After The Tears Dry
Downward Spiral

About the Author

Sandra K-Horn has worked in politics, education, and broadcast media. After teaching for thirty-one years, Sandra retired from teaching English and Communications at the high school level. During her teaching tenure, the Television Academy of Arts and Science awarded K-Horn and her students 12 High School Awards of Excellence. Time Warner awarded her Teacher of the Year in 2006 and 2008.

As she was teaching, she became concerned about teens and prescription drugs. This inspired her to write *The Rabbit Trap* to alert teens and their parents about the perils of using prescription drugs for entertainment or taking unprescribed medications for anxiety or stress. The *Eric Hoffer Award awarded The Rabbit Trap an honorable mention* in 2007. More magazine published her "Zip lining in Costa Rica" article in 2008.

In 2021, Ohioana Library featured *Downward Spiral (formerly The Rabbit Trap)* in its 15th Anniversary Festival. *After the Tears Dry* launched on July 12, 2022. Her first nonfiction, *Undercover, Becoming Street Smart in Central Ohio,* launched on November 1, 2022. It is a biography of two undercover police officers, one of whom is an advisor for her books.

She has attended The Midwest Writers and Central Ohio Fiction Writers Conferences. Sandra is a member of the Women's Fiction Writer's Association, Pitch 2 Publish, an international writing/publishing organization, and the Ohio

Branch of the National League of American Pen Women.

197

Copyright

The Springridge Incident is a work of fiction. All the characters, organizations, and events in this novel are either products of the author's imagination or are used fictitiously. No part of this novel may be reproduced in any form or by any electronic systems, without written permission by the author except for the use of brief quotations in a book review. Cover Design by GetFast.com

ISBN-13: 979-8-218-44283-5

9 798218 442835